TAHITI

by Marau Taaroa & Henry Adams

MEMOIRS OF ARII TAIMAI E
MARAMA OF EIMEO TERIIRERE OF TOOARAI
TERIINUI OF TAHITI
TAURAATUA I AMO

Henry Adams

CONTENTS

CHAPTER I

If the Papara family and people had any name, in European fashion, I suppose it would be Teva, for we are a clan, and Teva is our clan name. On the map of Tahiti the four southwest districts, from Papara to the isthmus, are always marked as Te Teva iuta, the inner Tevas, and the whole peninsula of Taiarapu, beyond the isthmus, is marked as Te Teva itai or outer Tevas. The island of Tahiti is shaped like an hour-glass or figure of 8; but as the natives knew neither hour-glasses nor figures, they used to call the island a fish, because it had a body and a tail. The head is the peninsula of Taiarapu, at its southernmost point, Matarufau, at the Pari, Pali, or cliff, which overhangs the sea there; identical, I suppose, with the English Palisade. The tail is at the northwest point of the main island, at Tataa, in Faaa or Tefana i Ahurai. From the head, at the Pari, over both coasts of the peninsula and across the isthmus of Taravao, along the west coast of the main island as far as the tail in Tefanai Ahurai, the Tevas and their connections held a sort of loose sway. The distance is not great to one used to travel, for the entire circuit of the island is but a hundred and ninety-one kilometres, making about a hundred and twenty miles, of which the peninsula counts seventy-two kilometres or forty-five miles. The Tevas and their connections held all the forty-five miles of sea-coast in Taiarapu and the whole western half of the main island, or about thirty-seven miles, from Taravao nearly to the edge of the modern town of Papeete. Fully eighty miles of the richest coast were more or less controlled by the Tevas, while all the other tribes in the island occupied hardly forty.

The interior is very mountainous and cut into ravines so deep and precipitous that no large number of people could live there. The whole population was crowded on the strip of land which runs like a low shelf round the greater part of the island, interrupted only in three or four places, as at the Pari, by cliffs directly overhanging the sea. On this strip, less than a hundred and twenty miles long, and varying from the bare cliff, without even a beach, to one or perhaps two miles in extreme width, where the larger streams cut out a few broader valleys, Cook found in 1774 a population that he could hardly trust himself to estimate. Modern writers, without a shadow of reason, have rejected his evidence, but all other evidence confirms it. In 1767 Wallis had been astonished at the numbers of the people, and not without reason, for while he was still warping his ship into Matavai Bay he was surrounded by swarms of war-canoes. "When the great guns began to fire, there were not less than three hundred canoes about the ship, having on board at least two thousand men; many thousands were also upon the shore, and more canoes coming from every quarter."

Already in 1774, when Cook made his second voyage, disease and war must have begun to reduce the population from what it had been when Wallis arrived in 1767; yet Cook saw, at Pare Arue, a fleet of one hundred and sixty large double canoes, attended by one hundred and seventy smaller double canoes, preparing to set out against the neighboring island of Eimeo. This fleet, he calculated, could not contain less than seven thousand seven hundred and sixty men, allowing forty to each large canoe and eight to the small ones, and it was the contingent of only two districts, Attahuru and Ahurai. Afterward the number increased, until, allowing forty men to each war-canoe and four to each of the smaller canoes which were to serve as transports, &c., the men exceeded nine thousand: "an astonishing number to be raised in four districts, and one of them, viz: Matavai, did not equip a fourth part of its fleet.... The number of war-canoes belonging to Attahourou and Ahopata [Paea and Patea] was an hundred and sixty, to Tettaha forty, and to Matavai ten.... If we suppose every district in the island, of which there are forty-three, to raise and equip the same number of war-canoes as Tettaha, we shall find by the estimate that the whole island can raise and equip one thousand seven hundred and twenty war-canoes and sixty-eight thousand able men, allowing forty men to each canoe; and as these cannot amount to above one-third part of the number of both sexes, children included, the whole island cannot contain less than two hundred and four thousand inhabitants; a number which at first sight exceeded my belief. But when I came to reflect on the vast swarms which appeared wherever we came, I was convinced that this estimate was not much if at all too great."

Cook was one of the most exact explorers that ever lived, and on this second voyage he had as a scientific companion another man as exact as himself, John Reinold Forster, the naturalist and intended historian of the voyage, who wrote a volume of "Observations" about it, and among many other careful studies made a particularly careful estimate of the population. He concluded that on a very moderate computation the main island contained eighty-one thousand, the peninsula of Taiarapu contained half as many, or forty thousand five hundred, and the adjacent island of Eimeo or Moorea half of that of Taiarapu, or twenty thousand two hundred and fifty; which made one hundred and forty-one thousand seven hundred and fifty for the whole population.

Another method of calculation might have been used. Attahuru and Tettaha -- that is, the Oropaa and Tefana i Ahurai -- produced two hundred war canoes, one hundred and sixty from the Oropaa, forty from Faaa, besides the attendant small canoes, representing, on the South Sea habit of computation, ten thousand men. Assuming that the whole of this region from Papeete to Papara, thirty-six kilometres, produced ten thousand fighting men, the entire island, one hundred and ninety-one kilometres, should have produced fifty-three thousand men. Cook, by averaging districts, estimated sixty-eight thousand. The estimate by miles of coast is probably the one used by the natives, for the proportion of forty to one hundred and sixty is that of Faaa to the Oropaa, along the beach, about seven kilometres to twenty-eight.

On one point, at least, Cook and Forster could hardly have been deceived. They saw and counted a fleet of two hundred and ten large double war-canoes collected for an attack on Eimeo. Throughout Polynesia, as far as I know, the natives estimated each large war-canoe as carrying fifty men, at least. Less than that number could hardly have managed these great double vessels, from sixty to a hundred feet long, with platforms, which Cook measured and drew in pictures, and which old men still remember. Any native would certainly say that a fleet of two hundred double war-canoes carried, in round numbers, ten thousand men. Cook's estimate of nine thousand was low. In Tonga, thirty years later, Mariner gave a force of five thousand men, besides a thousand women, for fifty large canoes, an average of more than a hundred to each canoe; and in one or two cases the Tahiti canoes held nearly two hundred men. Forster counted in the largest double canoes at Matavai one hundred and forty-four paddlers and eight steersmen, besides thirty warriors on the platform.

There cannot be a doubt that Cook knew quite well what he said when he estimated the force which set out against Eimeo, in 1774, at nine thousand men, drawn only from thirty-six kilometres of the coast. From this fact, which is perfectly well attested, we can form some idea of the population of Eimeo, and from this we can again make a guess at the population of the whole group. Eimeo or Moorea, as every one knows who has read Cook, or the Missionary relations, or Herman Melville's Omoo, is a small island, opposite Papeete and Faaa, with fantastic mountain peaks which, a dozen miles away or more, lend unreal and mysterious beauty to the sunset as we watch it from the Papeete shore. Eimeo is forty-eight kilometres in circumference, and now contains, or did contain in 1887, fifteen hundred and fifty-seven persons, all told, of whom about five hundred are men of military age, above fourteen and below sixty years. Eimeo is smaller in circumference than the peninsula of Taiarapu, in the proportion of forty-eight to seventy-two, but its proportion of cultivable land is larger; of thirteen thousand two hundred and thirty-seven hectares, three thousand five hundred are fit for cultivation and were cultivated in the past -- that is to say, about eight thousand six hundred and fifty acres. It is, in fact, one large extinct volcano, whose crater, in the centre, has become the richest and most beautiful valley in the South Seas, opening, through two magnificent bays, northward upon the ocean.

The army and fleet of 1774 were raised to attack not the whole island of Eimeo, but only the district on the north, on the bay of Opu-nohu, or Taloo Harbor, as it was often called. "They told us," said Forster, "that their fleet was intended to reduce the rebellious people of Eimeo (or York Island) and their chief Te-aree-tabonooee [Terii tapu nui] to obedience, adding that they would make the attack in a district of that island called Morrea." When Cook returned to Tahiti, in 1777 on his third voyage, he found that the people of Moorea "had made so stout a resistance that the fleet had returned without effecting much, and now another expedition was necessary." Cook himself visited Taloo Harbor in October, 1777, and saw Mahine, the chief of Opunohu, or, as he spelt it and as it is pronounced, Poonohoo. Mahine was only one of the four fighting chiefs of the island; Teriitapunui was another, and according to Cook, the war was waged by the Tahiti chiefs in order to support Teriitapunui against Mahine.

From this we know that a fleet and army of nine thousand men were not able to conquer Eimeo, or even a part of the small island. Mahine held his own, and must therefore have had a fighting strength nearly equal, if not superior, to his enemy. If one, or, at the most, two districts made such resistance, the whole island of Eimeo, with its forty-eight kilometres of coast and thirty-five hundred hectares of cultivated land, should have had a fighting strength at least one-third greater than the attacking districts of Faaa and Teoropaa, with their thirty-six kilometres. Evidently this was the case, since the army of Faaa and Oropaa failed to conquer one part of Eimeo, even with the aid of another part.

On this calculation Eimeo should have had a total number of about forty thousand inhabitants, and on the same scale Tahiti should have had one hundred and sixty thousand, which makes two hundred thousand in all, as Cook estimated it. At all events, one cannot resist the evidence that between one hundred and fifty thousand and two hundred thousand persons at the least were then living in these little islands where some twelve or thirteen thousand now exist. The population was known to be excessive even for a race so simple in its wants. A single bread-fruit tree was often owned by two or more families, who disputed each other's rights of property over the branches. Infanticide was habitual.

Taking the smaller number of one hundred and fifty thousand, and supposing that, on an average, every mile of coast supported a thousand persons, if the main island of Tahiti and its peninsula of Taiarapu contained a population of one hundred and twenty thousand people along its coast line of one hundred and twenty miles, the Tevas and their coanections must have numbered more than eighty thousand; but the four districts which belong to the inner Tevas -- Papara, Atimaono, Mataiea and Vaiari -- covering about thirty miles of coast, would, on the same scale, have numbered about thirty thousand only, and these are the districts which made the home of the Papara family whose chief was, when Wallis and Cook arrived, the head-chief -- Ariirahi -- of the Teva connection, or, as they thought, the king.

Every one who has tried to tell the story of Tahiti has had to struggle with this idea of kingship, and none has yet made it intelligible to Europeans. I shall not try, because the idea was so far from distinct in the islanders themselves that until one has dismissed from one's mind the notion of government such as Europeans conceived it, one must always misunderstand the South Seas. We believe ourselves to belong to the great Aryan race -- the race of Arii -- and our chiefs were Arii, not kings. I will not even use the word king, but, to escape the risk of misunderstanding, will speak of chiefs only by the native title of Arii, or, in the case of head-chiefs, Ariirahi -- Great Chiefs.

Whatever else the Ariirahi could or could not do, some of them had one right peculiar to their rank, and this was the right to wear the girdle of feathers, as much the symbol of their preeminence as the crown and sceptre of European royalty. In Tahiti the heads of two families had the right to wear the Maro-ura, or girdle of red feathers. These were the families of Vaiari and Punaauia. The

Vaiari head-chief was officially called Teriinui o Tahiti; the Punaauia, a woman, Tetuanui e Marua i te Rai. The Papara head-chief had alone the right to wear the girdle of yellow feathers, the Maro-tea. These head-chiefs were sacred; wherever they appeared, inferior Arii or chiefs stripped themselves to the waist as a sign of respect, and, as the very ground the Ariirahi stood on became theirs, they were always carried on a man's shoulders when they went abroad, that they might not acquire the property of their neighbors. Yet, sacred as they were, probably none -- whether Teriinui, Tetuanui or Teriirere -- preserved the sacred character throughout the entire island. They were sacred only where they were among their own people or connections by marriage. Cook saw Teriirere of Papara with his father and mother (Amo and Purea) at Matavai, which is in Haapape, not a Teva district; and he saw the district chiefs strip themselves at Teriirere's approach; but this was because of a connection between the families. I doubt whether Teriirere would ever have been taken beyond Haapape or to Hitiaa, for in most of the eastern districts he was a stranger, and had neither a seat in their Maraes nor a claim on the hospitality of their chiefs.

The distinguishing mark of the Tevas was their clanship. They alone in the islands looked on themselves as a clan, and had a sort of union, weak at all times, but still real enough to make them unpopular outside their own limits. The eight Teva districts recognized Teriirere or Temarii of Papara as their political head, although Teriinui o Tahiti, the Vaiari chief, was socially the superior, and Vehiatua of Taiarapu was sometimes politically the stronger. Whenever Teriirere i Tooarai, the chief of Papara, sent his messengers to call the Teva districts together, the districts came; but the summons was so peculiar that it needs a whole volume of explanation.

In the first place, the messengers were political personages, such as I never heard of elsewhere. They were under-chiefs -- latoai. How many latoai formerly belonged to Papara I do not know; but in our day there are two subdistricts of Papara, Faina and Oropaa, and Faina has eight latoai; Oropaa has six. The whole body of latoai in each district are known as Hiva, and to any one who cares for the beginnings of things they are the most interesting part of our old society, for the Hiva of Papara might have been the source of all modern notions -- Parliament, Civil Service, Army, Law Courts, Police, Aristocracy, Democracy, and Commune. The latoai were the chosen fighting chiefs or warriors, and they had, as a part of their functions, the duty of punishing or revenging insults offered to the head-chief; but they could also, and sometimes did, depose and exile a head-chief and name another or recall the old one. Their interference in this way makes one of the most dramatic motives in island history.

The messengers whom Teriirere i Tooarai sent to summon the Tevas were latoais or under-chiefs of Papara, and of three kinds: one messenger for the home district, one for the inner Tevas, and one for the outer Tevas. They bore an official name while on service; they inherited the position, and the office might be filled by any member of the family to represent the actual head.

The messenger that summoned the inner Tevas went to Vaiari, or, as it is commonly called, Papeari (Vai and Pape both mean water), to the head-chief Teriinui o Tahiti, who wore the Maro-ura, the girdle of red feathers, and was the older and socially superior branch of the Tevas. The messenger delivered his message not to Teriinui o Tahiti, but to Maheanuu i Farepua, the same man or woman under another title. Maheanuu then came to Papara with Teihotua of Mataiea and Teriifaatau of Atimaono, and these three chiefs, with Teriirere, made the four heads of the inner Tevas.

The third messenger went to Vehiatua i te Matai of Hui and Taia-rapu, and Vehiatua called for the chiefs of the outer Tevas. In calling out the clans the names of the districts were rarely used; the official names of the head-chiefs alone were enough, but these names were really titles of rank, and sound quite unpronounceable to any but a native. In Taiarapu, for example, the head-chiefs ot the district first called (Vairao and Toahotu, next the isthmus) were Teahahurifenua and Moeterauri; the head-chief of Tautira was Tetuanui haamarurai; of Pueu, the title was Tetuanui Maraetata; of Afaahiti, it was Tetuanui Moearu. These chiefs or chiefesses represented the four outer Tevas, and came to Papara when summoned by Teriirere i Tooarai.

The Tevas had a common cry or signal call:

Teva te ua, Teva te matai,

Teva te mamari, e mamari iti au na Ahurei.

Teva the rain, Teva the wind,

Teva the roe, the roe dear to Ahurei.

I suppose it means that Teva is strong and swift like rain and wind, and numerous like the roe of fish; but I do not know why Ahurei loved fish-roe.

At the time of Wallis's visit in 1767, Amo, or properly Tevahitua, was head-chief of Papara and of the Tevas; or rather his son Teriirere, born about 1762, was head-chief, and Amo exercised power as his guardian, according to the native custom which made the eldest child the head of the family immediately on its birth. Amo's power as head-chief depended much, on his good understanding with Vehiatua and the outer Tevas; but the power of a head chief was made up of so many elements and such shifting materials that nothing except the symbols could be reckoned upon as permanent. The name of Arii, or Ariirahi (head-chief) was much; the wearing of the Maro-tea or the Maro-ura was more; the seat in the Maraes was of great importance; the right to impose a Rahui or Taboo was essential; the power of calling the Tevas to conference or war was peculiar to the Papara head-chief; the military strength of the Tevas was irresistible if it could be united; but perhaps the most decisive part of every head-chief's influence was his family connection. Nowhere in the world was marriage a matter of more political and social consequence than in Tahiti. Women played an astonishing part in the history of the island. In the absence of sons, daughters inherited chieferies and property in the lands that went with the chief's names or titles, and these chiefesses in their own right were much the same sort of personages as female sovereigns in European history; they figured as prominently in island politics as Catherine of Russia, or Maria Theresa of Austria, or Marie Antoinette of France, or Marie Louise of Parma, in the politics of Europe. A chief-ess of this rank was as independent of her husband as of any other chief; she had her seat, or throne, in the Marae even to the exclusion of her husband; and if she were ambitious she might win or lose crowns for her children, as happened with Wallis's friend Oberea, our great-aunt Purea, and with her niece Tetuanui reiaiteatea, the mother of the first King Pomare.

The family connections of Papara extended almost round the island. The eight Teva districts, over which Papara had a sort of clan-headship, stretched from the Palisade of Taiarapu, at the extreme south of the island, to the border of Teoropaa, a large district lying next to Papara on the west coast. Teoropaa contained two divisions, now called Paea and Punaauia, covering some twenty miles of coast. Over these the family influence of Papara extended more decisively than over the outer Tevas of Taiarapu. Next beyond Punaauia came Faaa or Tefana i Ahurai, a very narrow district (the tail of the fish) and independent, though commonly allied with Papara. Turning the tail of the fish, the northwest corner of the island, next to Faaa came Pare, in which is the modern town of Papeete, formerly a mere village of the Porionuu, but now the capital of the French possessions in Oceania. Pare and its adjoining district Arue were called the Purionuu; they were under one chief and were independent of Papara. Beyond the Purionuu came the Te Aharoa, a wide region stretching down the whole east coast, where the Papara influence was weak, if not hostile. No great chiefs existed on that side of the island, which happened to be the side where the English and French ships appeared. Vehiatua in Taia-rapu was a great chief; so was the head of Vaiari and of Papara; so was Punaauia and Tefana i Ahurai; the chief of Pare Arue might be called important; but between the Purionuu and the isthmus of Taravao, forty-eight kilometres, the whole region called Te Aharoa contained no chiefery of the first class. Hitiaa alone was a considerable district, but its chief had not the right to the Maro-ura, and was never at the head of a great confederacy.

Thus the Tevas were not only strong in themselves and their connections, but also in the weakness of their rivals. The Papara head-chief was never head-chief of the whole island. When he called his dependent districts to war or feast or council, he called the inner and outer Tevas and the Oropaa, but not Tefana, the Purionuu or Teaha-roa. The kingship which Europeans insisted on attributing to him, or to any other head-chief who happened for the time to rival him, was never accepted by the natives until forced on them by European influence and arms; but the Tevas when united were always more than a match for the rest of the island.

CHAPTER II

Even the origin and meaning of the Teva name is lost. The word is more or less known in many different places and languages. Fiji has a small tribe or clan of Tevas, but these are said to be not Polynesian at all. Our Tevas claim by tradition a descent from the Shark God. Many generations ago a chief of Punaauia, named Te manutunuu, married a chiefess of Vaiari, named Hototu, and had a son, Terii te moanarau. At the birth of the child, the father, Te manutunuu, set out in his boat for the Paumotu islands to obtain red feathers (Ura) to make the royal Maro for the young prince.

So the story begins by taking for granted that before the first Teva existed, Punaauia and Vaiari had already their own chiefs and Maraes. The legend is clear in adding that the Marae of Punaauia was founded for this same young prince, Terii te moanarau, by his father, Te manutunuu, in order that he might wear in his own Marae the Maro-ura which was made of the feathers collected in this voyage to the Pau-motus. The name Punaauia is said to have come from the killing of a relation whose body had been rolled up as fish were rolled. The legend starts by assuming that Vaiari was the oldest family, with its Maraes, and that Punaauia was later in seniority and rank.

While Te manutunuu was absent on his long voyage to the Pau-motus, which required several months, a visitor appeared at Vaiari and of course had to be entertained by the chiefess. This visitor, our first ancestor, was what Europeans call a demi-god; he was only half human; the other half was fish, or shark-god; and he swam from the ocean, through the reef, into the Vaihiria river, where he came ashore, and introduced himself as Vari mataauhoe. The chiefess received him with the hospitality which was common to the legends of most oriental races, and Vari mataauhoe took up his residence with Hototu; but after their intimacy had lasted some time, one day, when they were together, Hototu's dog came into the house and showed his affection for his mistress by licking her face, or, as we should now say, kissing her, although in those days the word was unknown, for Polynesians never kissed each other, but only touched noses as an affectionate greeting. At this, the man-shark fell into a mood of reflection, and, after turning the subject in his mind, decided that the fault was so grave as to require him, as a person of refinement, to abandon Hototu: "You have been untrue to your husband with me," he told her; "you may be untrue to me with the dog."

Men have in all times been ingenious in their reasons for deserting women when tired of them, but, even in the South Seas and at that early day, this pretext must have been thought at least unusual, since it was preserved in legend. Unusual or not, it was enough for the man-shark, who walked off to the river, and turning into a fish again, swam out to sea. As he went on his way, or wherever he belonged, he met the canoe of the husband, Te manutunuu, returning from the Pau-motus, and stopped for a conversation with him. Te manutunuu, regretting to have lost the pleasure of a visit from so distinguished a guest, and obeying the rules of the somewhat excessive generosity which marked the island manners, invited Vari mataauhoe to return, but the man-shark civilly declined, giving as his excuse the reason that Hototu was too fond of dogs.

Perhaps this legend is as old as India and belongs to the common stock of world-myths; but, whatever its origin, its form seems to show that the natives looked on Vaiari as the source of their aristocracy. Not only did the Marae and Maro-ura of Punaauia claim descent from Vaiari, but Papara also followed closely, for when Vari mataauhoe was about leaving Hototu, he said to her: "You will bear me a child; if a girl, she will belong to you and take your name; but if a boy, you are to call him Teva; rain and wind will accompany his birth, and to whatever spot he goes, rain and wind will always foretell his coming. He is of the race of Arii rahi, and you are to build him a Marae which you are to call Mataoa (the two eyes of Tahiti), and there he is to wear the Marotea, and he must be known as the child of Ahurei (the wind that blows from Taiarapu.)"

A boy was born, and, as foretold, in rain and wind. The name of Teva was given to him; and Mataoa was built; and there Teva wore the Marotea. The Teva name came from this boy; but when or how it was given to the clan is unknown. Only we know that it must have been given by the Arii of Papara or Vaiari. To this day the Tevas seldom travel without rain and wind, so that they use the term Teva rarirari -- Teva wet always and everywhere.

Apart from these facts in regard to Teva's father and mother, little is known about him, but he must have been a very distinguished person, if the Vaiari people are to be believed, for they still point out the place where he lived as a child, his first bathing-place, and the different waters he fished as he came on his way toward Papara, and would feel insulted if any one should express a doubt of Teva's being a Vaiarian. In our family, we all admit not only that Teva was a branch of the Vaiari family, but that he wore the Maro-tea by right of that descent, and set up his Marae at Mataoa by transferring his stone seat or throne from the Marae of Farepua.

For the better understanding of any stranger who should read these memoirs, I should say here that every Arii or chief, great or small, had four properties belonging to his rank. None but those who have been mentioned could wear the Maro-ura, and only head-chiefs could order human sacrifices; but all equally possessed a Moua, or mount; an Outu, or point; a Tahua, or gathering-place, and a Marae, or temple. Arii, great and small, were too numerous to be told, and their Mouas, Outus, Tahuas, and Maraes were to be found at every mile of the coast, but the old and most important Maraes, from which the rest were mostly branches, numbered only about a dozen, and these must always be remembered, for they were the record of rank and the title of property throughout the island. Every one who has read Captain Cook's Voyages or any of the missionary books about Tahiti or Hawaii or the other Polynesian islands, knows that a Marae is a walled enclosure with an altar sacred to some God; but none of the books explain the social importance of the Marae, or that it represents, more than all else, the family. The God was a secondary affair, and even the right to human sacrifices had little to do with the Marae's rank. To natives, the family and the antiquity were alone seriously interesting. An aristocratic society, their religious arrangements were rigorously aristocratic, and a man's social position depended on his having a stone to sit upon within the Marae enclosure. Cook himself was greatly embarrassed when, on his departure from Raiatea in June, 1774, Oreo the chief asked him the name of his Marae. A man who had no Marae could be no chief, and Cook was regarded as a very great chief. His only resource was to give the name of his London parish. Forster, in answer to the same question entirely missed the point:

"Oreo's last request was for me to return; when he saw he could not obtain that promise, he asked the name of my Marai (burying-place). As strange a question as this was, I hesitated not a moment to tell him Stepney; the parish in which I live when in London. I was made to repeat it several times over till they could pronounce it; then Stepney Marai no Tote was echoed through an hundred mouths at once. I afterwards found the same question had been put to Mr Forster by a man on shore; but he gave a different and indeed more proper answer by saying no man who used the sea could say where he should be buried".

Vaiari, to begin with, had two very old and famous Maraes. One was called Farepua, and enjoyed the curious distinction of being the only Marae whose decorations were of Ura, or red feathers. The head-chief of Vaiari, as one of his titles, bore the name Maheanuu of Farepua. His other title of Teriinui belonged with the Marae called Tahiti. The name of Marae Tahiti has puzzled us all. Whether the Marae was named after the island, or the island after the Marae, or what the name meant in either case, no one knows. If the iti is a diminutive, as in the mysterious Hawaiiki, from which the New Zealanders came, perhaps the original name might be Taha-iti; or, if the terminal is hiti, it might mean only eastern, and point backward to some western Taa. In either case the word must have been taken at a very early time by Vaiari as a sort of property; Tahiti must have been an original Vaiari name, for, after other great chiefs had grown up as equals, no Vaiari chief, however proud his family might be, could, in the courtesy which marked the old social relations, have asserted himself to be the one great nobleman of the whole island -- Teriinui o Tahiti.

Papara, as has been told, took its Marae of Mataoa from Vaiari, and the chief of Papara was Teriirere or Temarii or Tauraatua i Mataoa by right of this descent; but the original Marae in the territory now known as Papara was on the small subdistrict called Amo, a mile from the sea and close under the mountains. The Marae of Amo was called Taputuarai; from this Marae a stone was taken to found the Marae of Tooarai near the shore; and close to the Marae of Tooarai, almost within the same enclosure, Purea and Amo built for their son Teriirere the great stone pyramid at which, as I shall tell in the course of my story, Captain Cook and Sir Joseph Banks wondered, on the point of Mahaiatea. Some of the principal names or titles of the chief of Papara, with their Maraes, were: Teriirere i Mahaiatea; Aromaiterai i Outuraumatooarai; Tuiterai i Taputuarai; but the chosen head, of the family had the right to all the Maraes. With each of these names and seats in the Marae went the lands attached to the title and the rights attached to the whole.

Paea or Attahuru was the next district to Papara, and belonged not to the Tevas, but to Teoropaa. Paea had two chief Maraes: Maraetaata and Teraiapiti. The next district, Punaauia, had a Marae of the same name, as I have already told. Faaa or Tefana had the Marae Ahurai. Pare Arue or the Purionuu had the Marae Tarahoi, in Arue, to which the Pomares belonged. The next district, Haapape, had the Marae Fararoi; and Hitiaa had the Marae Hitiaa.

These twelve Maraes of Tahiti-nui, or great Tahiti, were of course quite independent of those in the peninsula of Taiarapu -- Tahiti-iti, or little Tahiti. In Taiarapu the old districts were much changed by war, and the names have not kept their old meanings. Formerly the southern end of the peninsula, consisting of two districts, Taiarapu and Hui, formed one chiefery, called Teahupoo, whose head-chief bore the title Vehiatua, and whose Marae was Tapuanini or Matahihae. The northern part, Vairao and Afaahiti, had no common head, but the chief-ess of Vairao, Tetuau meretini, had the Marae Nuutere. The eastern part formerly contained a large and very powerful chiefery called Tautira, which was conquered and its chief's line. extinguished by Vehiatua. The great Marae of Tautira was supposed to be peculiarly sacred to the God Oro, a sort of Tahitian Osiris, to whom the human sacrifices were made.

Thanks to the Maraes, the social rank of chiefs in the South Seas was so well known or so easily learned that few serious mistakes could be possible. On this foundation genealogy grew into a science, and was the only science in the islands which could fairly claim rank with the intellectual work of Europe and Asia. Genealogy swallowed up history and made law a field of its own. Chiefs might wander off to far distant islands and be lost for generations, but if their descendant came back, and if he could prove his right to the seat in a family Marae, he was admitted to all the privileges and property which belonged to him by inheritance. On the other hand, if he failed in his proof, and turned out to be an impostor, he was put to death without mercy. Relationships were asserted and contested with the seriousness of legal titles, and were often matters of life and death. Every family kept its genealogy secret to protect itself from impostors, and every member of the family united to keep it pure. The most powerful chiefess in the island, like Purea or Marama or Tetuanui reiaiterai, was as free from her husband's control as any independent princess of Europe; she had as many lovers as she liked and no one made an objection; but she could not rear a child that was known to be not of chiefly origin. Every child born of such a connection was put to death the instant of its birth; and as Tahitians were little accustomed to secrecy in such matters, the lines of descent were probably purer than in Europe, where society was less simple in its methods.

All these bits of island custom are told only to show that our Papara family was probably, as the tradition says, a younger branch of the Vaiari family, and junior even to Punaauia. Yet Wallis found the Papara chief politically superior to both the families who wore the Maro-ura, and he had been so for many generations. At some time in the past a revolution had overthrown Vaiari and put Papara in its place, but while Papara took the political headship, it could not take the social superiority, for, as long as society should last, the Marae of Farepua must remain the older and superior over all the Maraes of Papara and the Tevas.

Here again tradition comes in to tell how Papara won the headship, but as usual tradition is indifferent to dates and details, joins together what was far apart, and cares only for what amuses it. As the story is told by the people to each other, the affair must have happened some twenty generations ago, when the head-chief over Vaiari and Mataiea was Huurimaavehi, and Papara was tributary to him. The chief of Papara was called Oro; not the God, to whom genealogies commonly ascend as the origin of human beings, but the chief of the small district of Amo, which I have already mentioned as having the original Marae of Taputuarai. Amo is now a forest of bread-fruit and cocoanut trees, but in those days it must have had a force of several hundred fighting men, and as it stood on the edge of Mataiea, guarding against attack, its chief was a great fighter.

Beautiful women were always a lively interest in the island society, and were beauties by profession. On great occasions they swam in the surf and were admired; before their houses their fathers made a sort of platform or terrace, called paepae, paved with flat stones, where the girl sat, and strangers stopped to look at her and discuss the whiteness of her skin or the roundness of her figure. Such a beauty was at that time the daughter of Panee of Amo, an intimate friend of Oro's father, Tiaau. Her reputation for beauty reached the ears of Hurimaavehi at Vaiari, as was to be expected, seeing that the places are only ten or fifteen miles apart, and the people, besides fighting, fishing, climbing the hills for Fei or wild plantains, and singing and dancing at all times, had little to do except to talk about each other. Hurimaavehi, like most Tahitian chiefs, had a fancy for handsome women, and he carried the girl away by stealth to Vaiari. Panee, the father, not knowing what had become of his daughter, sought her in every direction, and, stationing himself on the Mataiea boundary, questioned every one who passed, until one day two men came along, and he asked them where they were from:

"From Vaiari," they replied.

"How is Hurimaavehi and those who surround him?"

From question to question he came at last to his point:

"What new beauty have you in Vaiari?"

"Talk of beauties," the strangers answered; "a wonderful beauty has just appeared there, and belongs to Hurimaavehi."

"Is she well treated?"

"No; he has turned her over to the servants and the dogs and the pigs and the fish of the sea."

At this news Panee burst into a frenzy of rage, and rushing into Mataeia attacked every one he met, until he had killed five of Hurimaavehi's people; and to make the quarrel still more violent, he charged the two travelers with a message of insult for the Vaiari chief such as could be atoned for only by death. Then, having made an instant war certain, he hurried back to his friend Tiaau and told him what had happened. Both hastened to Oro to warn him that Hurimaavehi with his warriors was coming.

Oro was asleep, drowsy with kava, which, as every one knows, was the kind of intoxication Tahitian chiefs most loved, and when they most resented being disturbed. Only a great war-chief could throw off the influence of kava suddenly, to go into a fight; which shows how great a fighter Oro was, for he gave his orders at once. To one he said: "Climb the cocoanut tree and watch!" for the tallest palm was the watch-tower of the Tahiti village. To the other he said: "Hide yourself and your men in the Marae! When you see Hurimaavehi, beat him!" The wall of the Marae is still to be seen close by the foundations of the chief's house, covered with trees and lost in forest, and must have been not only a convenient hiding-place, but the only place in the nature of a fort in the neighborhood.

Oro's arrangements were quickly made. Among such close neighbors war was a sudden affair. A secret march by night along the beach, or in canoes along the shore, would bring a hostile force before morning the whole length of the island, from Taravao to Faaa. Many a district has been suddenly attacked and its people massacred, every house burned and every pig carried away, in a raid of a few hours. Generally an alarm of a few minutes was enough to call the warriors to arms, and to hurry the women and children away to the hills. The small chiefery of Amo, where this affair occurred, is close to the hills, and probably its warriors were collected in the Marae, and its women and children were in safety in the woods before Panee called from the top of his cocoanut tree that he could see the spears of the approaching warriors from Vaiari.

Oro's plan of battle succeeded. Hurimaavehi came, was attacked and beaten; but, from this point of the story, even we victors must allow that our tradition needs some little gloss. That Oro should have pursued the flying enemy was perhaps only what an energetic chief must have done in the case of so desperate a quarrel; but, in view of the force which Oro must have had with him to effect a conquest and the very considerable conquests he effected, a candid listener would like to know the Vaiari side of the story. Even a Papara school-girl, if she reads in her history-book the story of Appius Claudius or of Tarquin, would be a little surprised to find that she knew all about it, and that Papara had a Brutus and Virginius of its own quite as good as the Roman. The fight about a woman is the starting-point of all early popular revolutions and poetry; but as all of us, in our family, are descended from Vaiari as well as from Papara, we do ourselves no wrong by doubting whether, after all, the woman was not a pretext or even an invention to account for the outbreak of a plot. Oro behaved as though his plans were arranged beforehand, for he chased the Vaiari chief straight through his country, over several miles of hills not easy to cross if the people were hostile, until Hurimaavehi took refuge in the neighboring district of Hitiaa, thirty miles from the battle-field, while Oro seized each district as he passed through, and declared it subject to Papara.

Primitive people seem to have kept certain stock-stories, as one keeps pincushions to stick with pins, which represent the sharp points of their history and the names of their heroes; but the pins serve their purpose in the want of writing. Perhaps Vaiari and Hurimaavehi may have had a different story to tell, and may have thought that, when Papara had grown to be stronger than Vaiari, its chief challenged a quarrel, on any pretext that served his purpose, in order to make Papara the ruling district. If this was the true story, Vaiari was afterward revenged; but in either case this was what Oro did. The younger branch conquered the elder branch, and from that day the chiefs of Papara issued their summons to all the Tevas, and took the political headship of the clan.

According to the legend, Oro pushed his conquests even into Hitiaa, or into lands claimed by Teriitua, chief of Hitiaa; and when Teriitua interposed and stopped his advance, a dispute followed, Oro insisting on one boundary; Teriitua on another. They agreed to refer the decision to their Gods; but Oro took the precaution to hide his friend Aia in a hole near the line which he claimed, while Teriitua neglected to provide a voice for his Hitiaa oracle. When Teriitua called, his God did not answer; but when Oro called: "Is it here ?" his friend underground answered like an echo: "Here!" and the boundary was fixed and still remains at that point, securing to the Tevas entire control of the isthmus of Taravao.

This is the story of the rise of Papara as it is still told among the people. Something of the kind certainly did occur, and I know no reason why the tradition may not be true precisely as it stands.

MARAES.

Ahuahu	. . .	Papara.
Ahurai	. . .	Tefana.
Amaama	. . .	Papara.
Ativavau (Maraetaata)	. . .	Paea in Teoropaa.
Fanautaitahi	. . .	Eimeo.
Fareia	. . .	Eimeo.
Farepua	. . .	Vaiari.
Fareroi	. . .	Haapape.

Hitiaa	...	Hitiaa.
Mahaiatea	...	Papara.
Manunu	...	Papara.
Maraetaata	...	Ativavau in Paea.
Maruia	...	Papara.
Matahihae	...	Teahupoo.
Matairea	...	Afareaitu in Eimeo.
Mataoa	...	Papara.
Matarehn	...	Papara.
Natoofa	...	Afareaitu in Eimeo.
Nuurua	...	Varari in Eimeo.
Nuutere	...	Vairao.
Outuraumatooarai. (Tooarai).		
Poutini	...	(?) Punaauia.
Punaauia	...	Punaauia.
Punuatoofa	...	Toura? Eimeo.
Puteaio Tepuoteaio	...	Atitara in Paea
Raianaunau	...	Pare Arue.
Ravea	...	Tautira and Teahupoo.
Tahiti	...	Vaiari.
Tapuanini	...	Teahupoo.
Taputapuatea	...	Pare Arue, from Raiatea.
Taputuarai	...	Amo in Papara.
Tarahoi	...	Arue.
Tefano. Maraetefano	...	Haapiti in Eimeo.
Tepuote. (Puteaio).	...	Paea.

Teraiapiti

Tooari. Outuraumatooarai	. . .	Papara.
Tuturuarii	. . .	Punaauia.
Umarea	. . .	Afareaitu in Eimeo.
Vahitutautua	. . .	Vaiari.
Vaiotaha	. . .	Haapiti in Eimeo.

CHAPTER III

Eight generations ago, about the middle of the seventeenth century the next great revolution occurred, and again tradition says that it was caused by women. If one is to believe history, men never fought about themselves.

Yet the woman was hardly to blame for the misfortunes and overthrow of Tautira, which ended in shifting the centre of power among the Tevas. I have said that Tautira was a large and powerful chiefery on the eastern side of the peninsula Taiarapu, which was balanced by Teahupoo, another large chiefery at the southern end. If Cook and Forster were right in thinking that Taiarapu might contain at least forty thousand people, the chief of Tautira, whose authority extended over Pueu and the ancient district of Afaahiti, covering some twenty-five miles of coast from the isthmus of Taravao to the Palisade, must have controlled nearly twenty-five thousand persons, and have commanded an army of six or eight thousand men. He was certainly a great chief, equal to the chief of Papara in military power.

About the year 1650, Tavi was chief of Tautira, and prided himself on being as generous as he was strong. All chiefs were obliged to be generous, or they lost the respect and regard of their people; but Tavi was the most generous of all the chiefs of Tahiti. He had a wife, Taurua of Hitiaa, the most beautiful woman of her time, and a son. Tavihauroa.

The chief of Papara and head of the Tevas at that time was Tuiterai or Teuraiterai. Like Hurimaavehi of Papeari, Tuiterai could not hear of a handsome woman without wanting her; but Tavi's wife was a person of too much consequence to be approached except in the forms of courtesy required between chiefs, and therefore Tuiterai sent his messenger to Tavi to request the loan of his wife, with a formal pledge that she should be returned in seven days. In the Polynesian code of manners, such a request could not be refused without a quarrel. It could not even be evaded without creating ill-feeling that might end in trouble. Had Tuiterai asked for Tavi's child or anything else that he regarded as most precious, the gift would have to be made, subject of course to reciprocity, for every chief was bound to return as good a gift as he received. Tavi did not want to lend his wife, but his pride and perhaps his interest required the sacrifice, and with the best grace in the world, like the grand seigneur that he was, he sent her to Papara. Apparently she made no objection; if the husband was satisfied, the island code had nothing to say to the wife.

Taurua came to Papara, like a Polynesian queen of Sheba, and made her visit to Tuiterai, who immediately fell madly in love with her, showing it by some acts that were amusing, and by others that were too serious for us to laugh at quite heartily even after eight generations. One of his amusing acts was to take the name Arorua (Aro, breast; rua, two) as a compliment to Taurua's charms, and Tuiterai arorua he is called to this day. The more serious act was that, at the end of the week's visit, he broke his pledge to Tavi, and refused to return Tauroa to her husband. This was an outrage of the most grievous kind, such as he might perhaps have inflicted on a very low man -- a man fit only for a human sacrifice -- but not on a chief; least of all on a chief of equal rank with himself. It was a challenge of force; an act of war. Tuiterai did not attempt to excuse it except on the plea of his infatuation. The Tevas still sing the song of Tuiterai arorua replying to Tavi's messenger who came to demand Tauroa:

"Why should I give up Tauroa? I will not give her up -- I, Tuiterai of the six skies -- her, who has become to me like the Ura to my eyes, brought from Baratoa -- my dear treasure. I have treasured her, and I treasure her yet as the Uras of Faau, and I will not give her up now. No, I will not give her up. Why should I give her up? -- I, Tuiterai of the six skies -- her, who has become like the Uras of Raratoa."

This song is a famous bit of Teva history and literature, and yet I am not sure either of its text or its exact translation. I have given it as it is often sung, but nothing is more difficult than to render the exact meaning of such a language. The song, as the Tevas sing it, is made up of two separate parts; the first is Teuraiterai's refusal to surrender Taurua. The native text, with an attempt at literal translation, runs thus:

TEURAITERAI AND TAURUA.

E ore e pa iau. no fea e pa iau.

I will not give her up! Why should I give her up!

Teuraiterai ono rai ono. e ura piria mai tau orio.

I, Teuraiterai of the six skies! the Ura that clings to my eyes!

E ura ahuahu mai Raratoa mai e te ipo iti e.

The Ura, sunshine from Raratoa, my dear treasure.

E tahi arii haamoe ite ura here.

One king lulled to sleep his dear Ura.

Mai piti e mai faau. tau mate ono i aia.

Like two united. I should die without her.

Ruruu te rai ma fau hia

Tie up the heavens like a net.

Fau hia te rai mai ata. e ata pua e ata rai.

Tangle the clouds of the sky, the clouds of Pua.

Mahiti te pea ma te paora

Open the net, make me dry.

Paora te pa ma tuatini tuatini te pito i haafifi

Dry the thousand thousand bonds that unite us.

Anapea anapea ia mau maitai.

The net, the net holds well.

Poetry is not supposed in any language to have an exact equivalent in prose, and I do not pretend to give an English equivalent for anything Tahitian. Whatever these verses mean in prose, at all events they show that our great-ancestor Tuiterai arorua was regarded as an uncommonly arbitrary chief even by his own people, much as they may have admired an act which appealed to the sympathy of every true South Sea islander. Fortunately this story, at least, is too modern to be suspected of being a myth. Taurua of Tautira and Helen of Troy belonged to the same society; Tavi and Menelaus were relatives; the coincidence runs through every island in the South Seas, where no traveler has been able to keep the Odyssey out of his mind whenever he has approached a native village; but the truth of the Trojan story might be proved by that of Papara; for no sooner did Tuiterai's refusal reach Tautira than Tavi-Menelaus, acting up to his high reputation, summoned his warriors and sent them against Papara, with orders to destroy it and to kill its chief. Papara had no walls like those of Troy to stand a siege; its forces were beaten in battle. Tuiterai was taken, and Taurua recovered.

Among the score of wars fought in early societies about women, and then made the subjects of poetry or legend, the Tahitian variety has a charm of its own because its interest does not end as most of such stories end, with the revenge of the injured party. It should have ended in the usual way, and Tavi had intended to do what any Greek or Norse chief would have done: kill his rival and sack his villages; but the affair took another turn. Tuiterai was wounded, captured, and bound; but when his captors were about to kill him he remonstrated, not with any feeble appeal for mercy, but with the objection, much more forcible to a Polynesian, that a great chief like himself could not be put to death by an inferior. None but an equal could raise his hand against him. None but Tavi must kill Tuiterai.

Tavi's warriors, in spite of their orders, felt the force of the objection, which was, no doubt, in reality an appeal to religious fears, for Tuiterai, as head-chief of the Tevas, was a person of the most sacred character. They carried him, bound and blindfolded, along the shore, some thirty miles, to Tavi. The journey was long, and the wounded chief, feeling his strength fail, urged them on, and as they passed each stream he managed to dip his hand in the water to mark his progress, for he knew the touch of the water in every stream.

When Tavi learned that his warriors had brought Tuiterai alive, he reproached them for disobeying his orders. Even he found it hard to live up to his reputation. The pride of generosity had cost him his wife and a war; and still he must forfeit his character if he put Tuiterai to death with his own hand in his own house. The wars of Tahiti were as cruel and ferocious as the wars of any other early race, but such an act as this would have shocked Tahitian morality and decency. Tavi felt himself obliged to spare his rival's life, but between complete vengeance and complete mercy the law knew no interval. A chief spared was a guest and an equal. Tavi gave Tuiterai his life and his freedom and Taurua besides. The legend repeats his words in a song which is still sung, like the answer of Tuiterai to the demand for Taurua, as one of the best-known Teva ballads:

TAVI AND TEURAITERAI

A mau ra i te vahine ia Taurua.

Tou hoa ite ee. e matatarai maua e.

Taurua horo poipoi oe iau nei.

To aiai na pohe mai nei au ite ono.

Nau hoi oe i teie nei ra.

A mau ra ia Taurua tou hoa ite ee.

Matatarai mauai maua e.

"Take, then, your wife! Taurua! my friend! we are separated, she and I! Taurua, the morning star to me. For her beauty I would die. You were mine, but now -- take, then, Taurua! my friend! we are separated, she and I!"

Nevertheless, the overthrow of Papara was too serious a revolution not to affect the politics of the island. Tavi became by this triumph the most powerful chief in all Tahiti, and asserted his power by imposing a rahui for the benefit of his young son, Tavihauroa. A rahui was a great exercise of authority, and was more than royal in its claims. The rahui, which might last a year or more, was a sweeping order that everything produced during that time in the whole territory subject to the influence of the chief should be tabu or sacred to the young prince. Not a pig should be killed; not a tapa cloth or fine mat should be made; "not a cock should crow," except for the child; and at the end of the rahui, all was to belong to the infant.

Tavi's direct and full authority extended only over his own chiefery of Tautira, but by rank or courtesy, through his family connection or his influence it extended over the whole island, and only Eimeo or Moorea was exempt. A rahui was a form of corvée to which other great chiefs seldom willingly submitted; but even if a chief were himself anxious to avoid a war, which was the penalty of breaking it, his wife or his sisters or his relations were always ready to urge him to conspire against it. Tavi's chief rival was Vehiatua, head-chief of Tea-hupoo, which backs against Tautira on the south. Vehiatua had a daughter who had married the head-chief of Pare Arue, the district in the extreme north where the city of Papeete stands; and this daughter, Tetuaehuri, was about to give birth to a child.

This is the first appearance in history of the family which has since become famous and royal under the accidental, missionary title of Pomare. As every one knows, Pomare was merely one of several nicknames successively taken by Tunuieaite atua, the grandson of Tetuaehuri. Every Tahitian chief took such names, usually to commemorate something that happened to him, and very often out of regard for a child; but these nicknames were not permanent like the official titles that carried with them lands and rank. The official name of the chief of Parue Arue, Tetuaehuri's husband, was Taaroa manahune, who traced his descent from Fakaroa, an island of the Paumotus. In rank, Taaroa manahune stood in the third or fourth class -- at least, in the opinion of the Vaiari and Punaauia chiefs who wore the Maro-ura; of the Papara chief who wore the Maro-tea; of Vehiatua of Taiarapu, and Marama of Haapiti in the Moorea, and of Vaetua of Ahurai. Except as the husband of Tetuaehuri, he made no great figure. Ghiefesses like Tetuaehuri were apt to do much as they pleased when their husbands were less important than their fathers. Tetuaehuri was with child, and her midwives or attendants, or, as we now say, her medical advisers, told her that she must eat pig every day. If Vehiatua was consulted he gave his assent, for Tetuaehuri broke the rahui and eat the pig. Tavi acted at once as though this were a declaration of war by her father; he crossed with his warriors into Teahupoo and was totally defeated by Vehiatua.

The quarrel must have been unusually bitter, for this was one of the few instances where a great family was driven fairly out of the island. Vehiatua did not imitate Tavi in generosity, but seized his land. Some say that Tavi went to the Paumotus, but certainly after the war of the Rahui he was never again seen or heard of in Tahiti. His son, Tavi-hauroa, the cause of the disaster, came back and was protected by his old neighbors and relations, the chiefs of Hitiaa, Mataoae and Vaiari. By giving him land and servants they made up a small district for him, the modern Afaahiti, five or six miles of the coast beyond the isthmus of Taravao. He had also the names of Teriitua in Hitiaa and Terii oite-rai in Vaiari.

One day the unfortunate young chief was flying or racing his kite, a common amusement in ancient times when the men made kites as big as a house, and raced them against each other. The strong southeast trade wind which blows across the isthmus of Taravao carried the kite some miles to the westward, and he pursued it until it lodged in a tree within the Marae of Farepua in Vaiari. The high-priest happened to be conducting some sacred ceremony in the Marae, and at such a time the intrusion of a stranger was death. Terii oiterai climbed the tree to recover his kite, and was then and there instantly killed.

The extinction of this line must have been a serious matter for the island, because it gave to Vehiatua so great an increase of power as to make it a mere matter of time when he should do to Papara what Papara had done to Vaiari, and become the political head of the Tevas, and therefore the most powerful chief of the island. The Papara chief could escape the danger only by an alliance with Vehiatua, and accordingly in the next generation Vehiatua had for a wife Teeva Pirioi, an elder sister of the Papara chiefs Aromaiterai and Tuiterai Papara managed to retain its supremacy for that generation, but the danger was always there; the hour was sure to come, and so was the woman.

The revolution in Taiarapu is the starting-point of what we may call island history. It happened about a hundred years before Wallis discovered Tahiti; for the beautiful Taurua and Tetuaehuri were contemporaries, and while Taurua by her second marriage with the Papara chief, Tuiteral i arorua, became the source of our Papara family, Tetuaehuri by her marriage with Taaroa manahune became the source of the Pomares.

From this point our Papara genealogy seems clear. Amo of Papara, Cook's friend, was a gray-headed man in 1774, and his wife was five-and-forty in 1767; Amo was therefore born about 1720; since he was regarded by Cook as brother of Hapai or Teu, who must have been born as early as 1720. Amo's father, Tuiterai, must therefore have been born about 1690 or 1700; Tuiterai's father, Teriitahia, the son of Taurua, would be born between 1660 and 1670, which cannot have been very long after the date of the Rahui and the birth of Tetuaehuri's son.

Unfortunately these dates differ by two whole generations from the record of the Pomare genealogy. According to this, Tetuaehuri's son was Teu or Hapai, and lived until 1802, when he died, a very old man, well known for more than thirty years to all Europeans who visited Tahiti. He was about seventy years old in 1797, according to the misssionaries, who knew him intimately. He was supposed to be the oldest man in the island when he died, but no one seems to have supposed him to have been born before 1720. Even by shortening ten years each generation of the Papara genealogy, it cannot be made to coincide with the Pomares. Tetuaehuri should be not the mother but the great-grandmother, of Teu. Amo and Teu were contemporaries; their grandmothers should have been contemporaries; but, according to the genealogies, Teu's mother, Tetuaehuri, and Amo's great-grandmother, Taurua, were bearing their first children at about the same time. The Rahui, imposed after the birth of Taurua's first son, was broken by the birth of Tetuaehuri's first son.

Between the breaking of the Rahui and the arrival of Wallis in 1767, the Pare Arue family disappears, and I must leave them aside till I come to the generation of Amo and Purea, Teihotu and Vavea, Auri and Tetuaraenui, Tutaha, and the rest of Cook's friends. In the Papara family the intervening period was filled by a lively struggle between an elder and a younger branch -- an Aromaiterai and a Tuiterai -- which has left some pretty and graceful bits of family tradition.

The beautiful Taurua i Hitiaa, who had born her first son, Tavi-hauroa, to Tavi, bore a second son, Teriitahia, to Tuiterai of Papara. All these events in Taurua's life must have been crowded into a short period. Beauty does not last long in Tahiti. Taurua must have married; had her first son; gone to Papara; been recovered by Tavi's war with Tuiterai; been restored to Papara; and probably born her second son to Tuiterai, before the time of the Rahui war. This child, our ancestor in the sixth generation, was named Teriitahia i marama.

Teriitahia married a daughter of the chief of Vairao in Taiarapu, and had four children: two daughters and two sons. The two daughters were older than the two sons. The eldest, Teeva, married in Raiatea and left Tahiti. The second, Teeva Pirioi, as I have said, married the Vehiatua of her generation, and was usefully occupied in keeping peace on that side. The two sons were not so well employed.

CHAPTER IV

Aromaiterai and Tuiterai were the names of Teriitahia's two sons, and, if our genealogies are right, they must have been born, as I have said, between 1690 and 1700. Aromaiterai was the elder, and naturally claimed his father's position as head-chief. Tuiterai disputed the claim, and, if the family tradition is correct, his plea raised a question worth noticing in these days, when the study of primitive law has become a hobby.

Tuiterai's plea or defence seems to have turned on the idea that the eldest child, whether male or female, was the only heir who could set up an indefeasible right to the succession, and since the eldest child in this case, being a woman, had married and gone off to Raiatea, all the younger children had equal rights, and might with equal justice claim the position of head-chief.

This was one of the cases in which the sub-chiefs or Hiva must have been the judges, and although we know nothing about the reasons for their action or even the time when they acted, we do know that at one time or for a certain period they decided to send Aromaiterai away -- banish him, in fact -- and that they did it.

As usual, the memory of this revolution is preserved only by a song, but in this instance the poet was Aromaiterai himself, and the song is Aromaiterai's Lament. The Hiva had sent him out of the district and had placed him in a house at Mataoae, with an emphatic warning that he must not even tell the people of Mataoae who he was. Mataoae is not to be confounded with Mataoa, the Marae of Papara. Mataoae is a district on the southwest coast of Taiarapu, and a person standing on the beach there can see to the northwest, across twenty miles of water, the mountains behind Papara.

I do not know whether Papara is commonly thought to be one of the beautiful parts of Tahiti. I imagine not. Travelers can find so much that charms them elsewhere, and so much variety in the charm, as to make them indifferent to all scenery but the most impressive. Among a dozen books that have been written by visitors to the island, I am not sure that one of them, except Moerenhout, devotes a dozen words to Papara. To the Tevas and their chiefs, naturally, Papara is the world, and probably no part of the island compares with it for association, pride and poetry. Every point, field, valley, and hill retains a history and a legend. Purea's Marae of Mahaiatea still rises, a huge mass of loose coral, above the level of the plain. Aromaiterai at Mataoae could fix on the spot where his own Marae -- Teva's Marae -- of Mataoa invited him home, where in his time each of the two chiefs had a seat or throne on either side of the altar. At the outlet of a stream where the chiefery stands -- Terehe i Mataoa -- the reef is broken and falls away on either hand, and there in old days, when the shore swarmed with thousands of men and women caring for little but amusement, crowds were always in the water, riding the never-ending surf which seems nowhere else so much at home. Even now, in a cave, somewhere on the face of the precipice above the opening of the valley, Aromaiterai's skull is probably preserved, with those of other Aromaiterais, Tuiterais, Terii-reres, and Temariis, secreted so carefully that the secret is unknown even to us. Aromaiterai's Tianina -- his home-land by the chief's house -- is as familiar to the natives as their own faces. His Moua Tea-ratapu, and his Temaite or Temarua, the mountain side, are still a daily beauty to the Papara people. The stranger who drives along the road which now leads to Vaiari is still shown, three or four thousand feet above, on the slope of the distant mountain, outlined against the sky, the straggling line of trees which are called Aromaiterai's drove of pigs -- his Tiaapuaa, on the Mouarahi, the great mountain. Long white threads, hundreds of feet in perpendicular descent, mark the cascades on the green wall -- the Pari -- of the mountain. The dews or showers gather in the morning on the mountain-tops and spread the cloud -- Aromaiterai's cloak -- that shut them out from his sight.

According to the tradition, the unknown stranger who had taken his abode at Mataoae, when he came out of his house in the early morning, looked across the bay to the distant mountains behind Papara, and repeated his lament until the people divined his secret.

AROMAITERAI'S LAMENT.

Ei Mataoae au hio atu ai i tau fenua ite Tianina.

Ite moua ra o Tearatapu te peho i Temaite

Tiaa puaa ite moua rahi

Ua tahe te hupe ite moua

Ua ho ra hia tau ahu.

Terara ua e. e ore oe e iriti ae

Ia hio atu au ite moua rahi ra

Aue le pare i mapuhi e tau fenua iti e

Te pahu taimai o nia o Fareura

E iriti hia mai te matai o te toa

Ei tahirihiri no te arii no Aromaiterai.

Ite huru o tou aia.

"From Mataoae I look toward my land Tetianina, the mount Tearatapu, the valley Temaite, my drove of pigs on Mouarahi, the great mountain. Mist hides the mountain. My cloak is spread. Oh that the rain clear away, that I may see the great mountain! Aue! alas! the wall of Mapuhi, dear land of mine!

"The drums that sound above Fareura draw to me the winds of the south for a fan to fan the chief Aromaiterai. [I long for] the sight of my home."

Nothing could well be simpler, and if perfect simplicity is a beauty or homesickness is poetic, even a foreigner who never has seen or heard of Papara can understand that the Tevas, who are not in the least introspective and who never analyze their sensations or read Browning or Wordsworth, should ask no more. "There is my field!" Aromaiterai laments; "There is my hill! there is my mountain-grove, my drove of pigs! How I wish I were there!" Aromaiterai used no more words; but each word calls up a picture to the singer, and what more can any poet do?

Europeans, who are puzzled to understand what the early races mean by poetry, look for the rhythm as likely to explain a secret which they cannot guess from the sense of the words; but Polynesian rhythm is, if anything, rather more unintelligible to European ears than the images which are presented by the words. Tahitian poetry has rhythm, but it is chiefly caused by closing each strophe or stanza by an artificial, long-drawn, é-é-é-é! The song is sung with such rapidity of articulation that no European can approach it or even represent it in musical notation, and as for the sounds themselves, one can best judge of them by glancing at the native words.

Other Polynesian dialects have a way of using indifferently k or t. Tahiti is then Kahiki; Tamehameha, the king of Hawaii, became Kame-hameha. We use t always, and the l becomes r in Tahitian. The Mariage de Loti is properly the Mariage de Roti. The dialect is never guttural or harsh; the verses seem to run off the tip of the tongue with a rapidity impossible to any one but a native. Singing was as natural as talking, and one danced as naturally as one walked.

Now that I am on the subject of family poetry, I must give here another song which was made by Taura atua i amo, and is still a favorite with the Tevas, the more because it is a love-song. The name of Tauraatua belongs to the little district of Amo, in Papara, and has been one of the family names for so many centuries that I cannot say which of the Tauras was the poet; but the motive of the poem was probably common to all of them, for it was common enough throughout the world. The young chief was in love with a girl of lower rank, who lived at the Ruaroa, a cluster of houses near the beach, by the Marae of Mataoa at the western end of Papara. The paepae, as I have said, was the paved. terrace before the house. He calls his mistress Marae-ura in the song. Illegitimate connections were common enough in all societies, but in one way Europe was less rigid than Tahiti in its rules, not of morals, but of marriage. Unequal marriages were not merely unusual; they were impossible. The family would not permit them even in the case of the most powerful chief that ever lived. Illegitimacy was common, but if there was danger that a low-born child should ever take inheritance in the family, the child was put to death. Even if the connection threatened to be inconvenient, the family or the Hiva would interpose and insist on the chiefs return to his own place. This is the subject of Tauraatua's song. The messenger, called the bird Uriri, had come to the Ruaroa, where Taura was living with his mistress, and brought the order for him to return to Papara. The song begins by repeating the message, and closes by a verse in which the lover, who is obliged to leave his mistress, pushes aside the leaves to catch sight of her bathing on the beach.

LAMENT OF TAURAATUA.

Taura atua te noho maira i tona ra paepae i te pacpaeroa

E uriri iti au e rere i te Ruaroa

E fenua Papara ite rai rumaruma

E haere a i Teva tena teaia tei Papara to fenua ura e

Moua tei nia Moua Tamaiti

E Outu tei tai Outu manomano te faarii raa ia Teriirere i outu rau ma Tooarai

E tii na vau e turai e atu i teniau para o te Ruaroa e

Ia vai noa mai nau i puu rii o Maraeura tei tai e

"Taura atua lives at the paepae of the paepaeroa

The little Uriri flies to the Ruaroa, for him the loved:

'Come back to Papara, the heavy-leaved;

Come back to Teva, your home, your Papara, the golden land;

Your Moua, the Moua Tamaiti above;

Your Outu, the Outu Manomano on the shore,

The throne of Teriirere of Tooarai.'

Then let me go and bend aside the golden leaves of the Ruaroa

That I may see those two buds of Marae-ura on the shore."

Paraphrase is all one can try for, where languages are so hopelessly different. The native figures have no meaning in English. The Uriri passes the power of translation. Perhaps rumaruma may convey an idea of branches weighed down by their leaves, but the leaves of the bread-fruit and the palm are something different from those of the oak and beech. The Ura -- the reddish feathers of the parrot or parroquet -- may perhaps pass for orange-red or golden; but local terms like Pae-paeroa, Moua, Outu, and the like, need a long education to slip gracefully on the tongue or through the mind.

I do not know what became of Aromaiterai and Tuiterai, or when they died, but they left behind them one of the most complicated puzzles in genealogy that ever perplexed a succession. I will try to finish with the Aromaiterais and clear them out of the way before going on with the main stream of our family history in the Tuiterais; but this is not easy, because the course of the main stream meanders freely between the two. No doubt Tuiterai did drive out Aromaiterai, about 1730, and when Wallis arrived, in 1767, Tuiterai's son, Amo, or Tevahitua i Patea i Tooarai, still held the chiefs authority and headship over the whole island except a few districts; but Aromaiterai had married a wife, Teraha, and had two children: a daughter, Tetuanui, and a son, Aromaiterai who married his first cousin, sister of Amo. These two children carried on the elder branch of the family till it reaches us.

The daughter, Tetuanui, was the channel through which the Aromaiterai name and lands came back to us at last through my mother, Marama. The Table II shows how, in the failure of males, the line passed through Teraiefa of Maraetaata, wife of Marama of Haapiti, to their son Marama, and through him to his daughter, the greatest chiefess and heiress of her day, whose marriage to Tuiterai's heir, Tapua taaroa of Papara, reunited the Aromaiterai and Tuiterai branches in myself, Ariitaimai, who am Aromaiterai and Tuiterai in one.

CHAPTER V

The younger Tuiterai, whose birth I have ventured to date, like that of his brother Aromaiterai, between the years 1690 and 1700, married Teroroeora i Fareroi; that is to say, a daughter of the chief of Haapape; and this was the relationship which made the Papara family at home in Haapape when Wallis and Cook appeared there. The marriage must have taken place about 1720.

The eldest son of Tuiterai and Teroroeora or Aroroerua was Tevahitua i Patea, who must have been born about 1720-1725. Besides this son, Tevahitua, there was the daughter Tetuaunurau, already mentioned as marrying her cousin Aromaiterai; there was a Tauraatua of whom we know nothing; and there was another son Manea, from whom we are directly descended in the fourth generation.

Tevahitua seems to have been recognized as head-chief of the Tevas, although his cousin and brother-in law Aromaiterai may have had an equal seat in the Marae of Mataoa and quite as much influence with the Hiva. The only tradition left in the family from this long division in the last century is that there were always at Papara an Aromaiterai and a Tuiterai, and that they never could agree. Probably they agreed still less after Tevahitua's marriage, which must have taken place about 1750.

If a family must be ruined by a woman, perhaps it may as well be ruined thoroughly and brilliantly by a woman who makes it famous. Te vahine Airorotua i Ahurai i Farepua, and of most of the other highest connections in the island, was a very great lady. Standards of social rank differ a little in different countries and times, but in any country or time a woman would meet with consideration when she and her husband could control a hundred thousand people; when she could build a pyramid for her child, and take for him the produce of a swarming country; when she was handsome, with manners equal to the standard of countries where the manners of Europe would be considered barbarous; and finally, when she had an unbroken descent from chiefs as far back as human society existed; and the consideration would not be the less because, like a large proportion of the more highly educated ladies and gentlemen of Europe, her views on some points of morality were lax and her later career disastrous.

Airorotua, familiarly called Purea, was a daughter of Terii vaetua, chief of Tefana i Ahurai or Faaa, the tail of the fish, close to the modern Papeete and partly including it. The district of Faaa, though it contained only about seven miles of seacoast, was for many reasons very important. It stood, as an independent little nation, between the great Teva alliance on the south, the Porionuu and te Aharoa on the east, and the large island of Eimeo or Moorea, some twelve miles to the west. As Tefana leaned toward Papara or against it, the chiefs of Papara were apt to be less anxious about their enemies or more anxious to win friends. At the time when Amo married Purea, in the middle of the last century, Tefana was particularly strong in its connections.

Terii vaetua, Purea's father, had married one of the Vaiari family -- Te vahine Airoro anaa te arii ote maevarau of Vaiari, marae Farepua, born literally in the purple or scarlet of the Ura. They had seven children: (1) Tepau i Ahurai, known in the English books of travel as Tubourai Tamaide; (2) Terai mateata; (3) Hituterai; (4) Te vahine Airorotua, or Oberea, Berea, Purea; (5) Teihotu; (6) Auri; (7) Mareiti. Of these seven children three were persons of no small concern to us -- Purea, Teihotu, and Auri. Purea married the chief of Papara and became mother of Teriirere; Teihotu married Vavea of Nuurua and was grandfather of King Pomare; Auri married Tetuaraenui of the Punaauia and Vaiari families and was grandfather of Marama. Thus King Pomare was second cousin of my mother, Marama Arii manihinihi, and as in Tahiti cousins are regarded as brothers and sisters, Pomare always called my mother sister, which had a curious effect on our lives and fortunes.

With such connections as her father and mother and husband gave her, Purea had no serious rival in the island, and when her son Teriirere was born, somewhere about the year 1762, he became at once the most important person in the world in the eyes of his mother and of Tahiti. The son always superseded the father, whose authority after the birth of a child was merely that of guardian. As often happened, Tevahitua took a new name from the child, and called himself Amo, the winker, from a habit of winking which seems to have amused him in the infant Teriirere. The same cause that superseded the father gave the mother often an increase of influence and freedom from restraint. Purea, after the birth of Teriirere, was emancipated, and the relation betwen her and Amo was from that time a political rather than a domestic one. They were united only in the interests of Teriirere.

They then asserted the child's supremacy by undertaking what no other great chief had ever attempted, and what still strikes us with astonishment as it struck Captain Cook and Sir Joseph Banks in 1769. They not only imposed a general Rahui for the child's benefit, as Tavi of Tautira did for his unfortunate son a hundred years before; but they also began a new Marae for Teriirere, in which he was to wear the Maro, and they set their people to work on the enormous task of piling up the pyramid at Mahaiatea which was an exhibition of pride without a parallel in Polynesia.

This was more than Purea's female relations could bear, and it set society in a ferment. The island custom provided more than one way of dealing with pride. Though Purea and Teriirere were admitted to be political superiors, they were socially no better than their cousins, and custom required that if during a Rahui any relative or guest of equal rank should come to visit the chief who had imposed it, the Rahui was broken, and the guest received by courtesy all that the Rahui had produced. Such an attempt to break the Rahui was of course an act which could not be ventured by any ordinary chief within the direct control of Papara; but Tefana i Ahurai was independent, and if Purea's own family chose to set up such a claim, Purea would resist it at her peril. Not even she could afford such a quarrel.

The first person who undertook to break the Rahui was probably Purea's sister-in-law, no doubt the wife or widow of Teihotu, on behalf of her son, Terii vaetua. She set out from Faaa in her double-canoe, with the house or tent, called fare-oa, in the prow, which only head-chiefs could use; and a crew of fifty men or more paddled this barge of state, with all the show of a royal ceremony, along the coast to Papara, some twenty miles away, until, opposite to the Point of Mahaiatea, they turned in to an opening in the reef which had on some pretext become sacred, and was known as the sacred pass, through which only sacred chiefs might go. Purea was then living on the Point, and probably was superintending the work on her great Marae. She came out on the beach, and as the double canoe, with its royal tent, passed through the opening and drew towards the land she hailed it:

"Who dares venture through the sacred pass? Know they not that the Tevas are under the sacred Rahui for Teriirere i Tooarai? Not even the cocks may crow or the ocean storm."

"It is Terii vaetua, Arii of Ahurai"

"How many more royal heads can there be? I know none but Teriirere i Tooarai. Down with your tent!"

The Ahurai chiefess wept and cut her head with the shark's tooth till blood flowed down her face, which was the custom of women in sign of great emotion, and meant in this instance revenge as well as grief; but Purea was inexorable, and Terii vaetua was obliged to turn round and go home like any ordinary stranger.

The quarrel, once begun, was extended by another of the Ahurai family, a woman who proved to be more than Purea's equal in most forms of energy. She was Purea's niece, the daughter of Teihotu and sister of the insulted Terii vaetua. Her name was Tetuanui rea i te Raiatea, and she was or became the wife of Tunuieaiteatua i Tarahoi, Cook's friend Otoo, and the missionaries' friend Pomare. A very famous woman in Tahitian history, much talked about by Captain Bligh in 1788 and by the missionaries as Iddeah, Tetuanui i Nuurua was not even mentioned by Wallis or Cook, although the latter, in 1774, frequently mentions "Tarevatoo, the king's younger brother," whom I take to be Terii vaetua, the king's brother-in-law, who had begun the attempt to break the Rahui. Indeed, Cook never saw even Pomare until August, 1773, when Pomare was already thirty years old.

After the repulse of Terii vaetua, this sister undertook to pursue the quarrel. The matter had become uncommonly serious, for a feud between Papara and Ahurai might upset the whole island. Nothing more would then be needed to overthrow the Papara supremacy than the alliance of Ahurai and the Purionuu with Vehiatua, whose fortunes had been made a hundred years before by a similar combination to break a similar Rahui. Tradition has preserved the precise words used by the family to avert the peril into which Purea's pride and temper were pushing them.

Tetuanui in her turn made her appearance in the state canoe off the point of Mahaiatea, and as she approached the beach was received by Purea with the same order, "Down with your tent!" Tetuanui came ashore and sat on the beach and cut her head with the shark's tooth till the blood flowed down into a hole she dug to receive it. This was her protest in form; an appeal to blood. Unless it were wiped away it must be atoned by blood.

Then the high-priest Manea interposed. Manea was Amo's younger brother, from whom we are directly descended in the fourth generation, and probably we owe our existence in a double sense to him, for his act wiped out the blood-feud as far as his own descendants were concerned.

"Hush, Purea! Whence is the saying, 'The pahus (drums) of Ma-tairea call Tetunai for a Maro-ura for Teriirere i Tooarai. Where wilt thou wear the Maro-ura? In Nuura and Ahurai. One end of the Maro holds the Purionuu; the other end the Tevas; the whole holds the Oropaa.'"

Manea quoted the maxim of family statecraft in vain. Purea replied only that she was going to allow no rivalry to her son. "I recognize no head here but that of Teriirere." Then Manea dried the blood of Tetuanui with a cloth, wiping away the feud as far as he was concerned; and so long are these things remembered that forty years afterwards, when the Purionuu savagely raided Papara, Manea's great-grandchildren were supposed to have been spared in memory of Manea's act.

This scene must have occurred at about the time when Wallis discovered the island, and had he taken forty-eight hours to make the visit to Papara which Purea invited him to make, perhaps he might have seen the preparations for the great feast at which Teriirere i Tooarai was to wear the Maro-ura for the first time in his great new Marae at Mahaiatea. Thus far I have had to depend mainly on tradition, but here Captain Wallis and Captain Cook begin their story from the European stand-point.

CHAPTER VI

On the 18th of June, 1767, Captain Samuel Wallis, on a voyage of discovery round the world in H. M. Ship "Dolphin," first saw the island of Tahiti, or, as he called it, Otaheite. The story was told in Hawkesworth's Collection of Voyages, and has been told over and over again, for the world never tired of reading it; but I, who have lived in Tahiti all my life and know the tale by heart, shall not repeat it, except so far as it concerns me and my family; and it does so, closely, in the part which at the time most delighted Europe. I must start by saying that all our exact knowledge of dates in the history of the island begins with June 24, 1767 when Wallis warped his ship into the bay of Matavai, in the district of Haapape, the most northerly point of the island, where two years afterwards Captain Cook selected his station for observing the transit of Venus and gave to the projecting spit of land the name of Point Venus, which it still bears. The same day occurred the well-known battle, which was renewed June 26, and which ended in the defeat of the natives and sudden friendship for their new European acquaintances; yet even after the partial opening of relations, Wallis remained a whole fortnight in Matavai Bay, but no chief came near him, and the common people were not allowed to approach the ship or the boats in any considerable number, until at length, on Saturday, July 11, a woman came on board whose appearance gave to Wallis's narrative an air of romance so charmingly old fashioned that any words but his own would spoil it.

"On Saturday, the 11th, in the afternoon, the gunner came on board with a tall woman, who seemed to be about five-and-forty years of age, of a pleasing countenance and majestic deportment. He told me that she was but just corne into that part of the country, and that seeing great respect paid her by the rest of the natives, he had made her some presents; in return for which she had invited him to her house, which was about two miles up the valley, and given him some large hogs; after which she returned with him to the watering place and expressed a desire to go on board the ship, in which he had thought it proper, on all accounts, that she should be gratified. She seemed to be under no restraint, either from diffidence or fear, when she first came into the ship, and she behaved all the while she was on board with an easy freedom that always distinguishes conscious superiority and habitual command. I gave her, a large blue mantle that reached from her shoulders to her feet, which I threw over her, and tied on with ribands; I gave her also a looking-glass, beads of several sorts, and many other things, which she accepted with a very good grace and much pleasure. She took notice that I had been ill, and pointed to the shore. I understood that she meant I should go thither to perfect my recovery, and I made signs that I would go thither the next morning. When she intimated an inclination to return, I ordered the gunner to go with her, who, having set her on shore, attended her to her habitation, which he described as being very large and well built. He said that in this house she had many guards and domestics, and that she had another at a little distance which was enclosed in lattice-work."

This visit first opened the island to the Englishmen, as Wallis instantly noticed; but he was so much more interested in his introduction into good native society that he quite lost sight of politics. From this moment until he sailed from the island, July 27, his narrative ran almost wholly on the subject of "my princess, or rather queen," until it ended in a burst of sentiment which, as far as I can learn, stands by itself in the literature of official reports as the only case of an English naval captain recording tears as part of his scientific emotions.

"The next morning (Sunday, July 12)," continued Captain Wallis, "I went on shore for the first time, and my princess, or rather queen, for such by her authority she appeared to be, soon after came to me, followed by many of her attendants. As she perceived that my disorder had left me very weak, she ordered her people to take me in their arms and carry me not only over the river, but all the way to her house, and observing that some of the people who were with me, particularly the first lieutenant and purser, had also been sick, she caused them also to be carried in the same manner, and a guard, which I had ordered out upon the occasion, followed. In our way, a vast multitude crowded about us, but upon her waiving her hand, without speaking a word, they withdrew, and left us a free passage. When we approached near her house, a great number of both sexes came out to meet her; these she presented to me, after having intimated by signs that they were her relations, and, having taken hold of my hand, she made them Kiss it."

In Wallis's narrative this scene is illustrated by a large engraved drawing which makes a charming picture of everything native contrasting with the ludicrous effect of the English uniforms and attitudes. Most of the details seem fairly correct and carefully done; the long native house with its thatched roof is still common in the islands; the so-called queen, looking very young and delicate, with a long dress of native tapa, is followed by her women, stripped to the waist, and these by men in attitudes ot welcome.

"We then entered the house, which covered a piece of ground three hundred and twenty-seven feet long and forty-two feet broad. It consisted of a roof thatched with palm leaves, and raised upon thirty-nine pillars on each side and fourteen in the middle. The ridge of the thatch on the inside was thirty feet high, and the sides of the house, to the edge of the roof, were twelve feet high, all below the roof being open."

The house was no doubt the Fare-hau, or Council-house, of the district of Haapape, and the princess, as Wallis called her, who did not belong to Haapape but to quite another part of the island, was herself a guest, whose presence there was due to her relationship with the chief.

"As soon as we entered the house, she made us sit down, and then calling four young girls, she assisted them to take off my shoes, draw down my stockings, and pull off my coat, and then directed them to smooth down the skin and gently chafe it with their hands. Having continued it for about half an hour, they dressed us again, but in this they were, as may easily be imagined, very awkward. I found great benefit, however, from the chafing, and so did the lieutenant and the purser. After a little time our generous benefactress ordered some bales of Indian cloth to be brought out, with which she clothed me and all that were with me, according to the fashion of the country. At first I declined the acceptance of this favor, but being unwilling not to seem pleased with what was intended to please me, I acquiesced. When we went away, she ordered a very large sow, big with young, to be taken down to the boat, and accompanied us thither herself. She had given directions to her people to carry me, as they had done when I came, but as I chose rather to walk, she took me by the arm, and whenever we came to a plash of water or dirt, she lifted me over with as little trouble as it would have cost me to have lifted over a child if I had been well."

From this time Captain Wallis as well as his sailors became bewitched with the island, and especially by the women, who, according to his account as given by Hawkesworth, "are all handsome, and some of them extremely beautiful." The queen sent him scores of pigs and fowls, with bread-fruit, bananas, cocoanuts and other fruit in large quantities, and every few days came herself on board to see him.

"On the 21st the queen came again on board, and brought several large hogs as a present, for which, as usual, she would accept of no return. When she was about to leave the ship, she expressed a desire that I should go on shore with her, to which I consented, taking several of the officers with me. When we arrived at her house she made us all sit down, and taking off my hat she tied to it a bunch or tuft of feathers of various colors, such as I had seen no person on shore wear but herself, which produced by no means a disagreeable effect. She also tied round my hat and the hats of those who were with me wreaths of braided or plaited hair, and gave us to understand that both the hair and workmanship were her own; she also presented us with some mats that were very curiously wrought. In the evening she accompanied us back to the beach, and when we were getting into the boat she put on board a fine large sow, big with young, and a great quantity of fruit. As we were parting I made signs that I should quit the island in seven days. She immediately comprehended my meaning, and made signs that I should stay twenty days; that I should go two days journey into the country, stay there a few days, bring down plenty of hogs and poultry, and after that leave the island. I again made signs that I must go in seven days; upon which she burst into tears, and it was not without great difficulty that she was pacified."

The queen, or properly the chiefess, was no doubt inviting Wallis to visit her own district, and perhaps may have had political reasons, which Wallis did not divine, for the disappointment she showed so strongly. Wallis's refusal has cost us an irreparable loss in our history. She came aboard again July 25, and stayed till evening:

"As she was going over the ship's side she asked, by signs, whether I still persisted in my resolution of leaving the island at the time I had fixed; and when I made her understand that it was impossible I should stay longer, she expressed her regret by a flood of tears which for a while took away her speech. As soon as her passion subsided she told me that she would come on board again the next day, and thus we parted."

The day of separation came quickly, and at daybreak, July 27, the "Dolphin" was ready for sea. The whole beach was covered with people, among them the queen, who wished to go aboard in the ship's boat, which was taking off the last water-casks and her farewell presents; but, as the officer had received orders not to bring off natives in his boats, the queen launched a double canoe and was brought to the ship by her own people.

"The queen came on board, but not being able to speak, she sat down and gave vent to her passion by weeping. After she had been on board about an hour, a breeze springing up, we weighed anchor and made sail. Finding it now necessary to return into her canoe, she embraced us all in the most affectionate manner and with many tears; all her attendants also expressed great sorrow at our departure. Soon after it fell calm and I sent the boats ahead to tow, upon which all the canoes returned to the ship, and that which had the queen on board came up to the gun-room port, where her people made it fast. In a few minutes she came into the bow of her canoe, where she sat weeping with inconsolable sorrow. I gave her many things which I thought would be of great use to her, and some for ornament; she silently accepted of all, but took little notice of anything. About ten o'clock we were got without the reef, and, a fresh breeze springing up, our Indian friends, and particularly the queen, once more bade us farewell, with such tenderness of affection and grief as filled both my heart and my eyes."

Wallis did not know the name of his queen, or what her true rank was, or from what part of the island she came; nor did Bougainville, who touched at Hitiaa, on the eastern side of Tahiti, only eight months afterward, in April, 1768, remain long enough to see much of the place or the people; but both these explorers returned to Europe with such glowing accounts of Tahiti as created lively interest. At that moment Europe, and especially France, happened to be looking for some bright example of what man had been, or might be, in a state of nature, and the philosophers seized on Tahiti to prove that, if man would only rid himself of restraints, he would be happy. This is an account of our family, not a history of the island, and I am not well acquainted even with the names of the philosophers who brought about the French Revolution by trying to apply to France the state of nature which Bougainville described in what he called the island of New Cytherea; but I know that Diderot wrote a "Supplement to Bougainville's Travels" in the form of a dialogue between the ship's chaplain and a Tahitian supposed to be named Orou, and that Orou overwhelmed the chaplain by showing the superiority of Tahiti over Paris, and the immorality of constancy in marriage.

One of my friends has pointed out to me another French book, printed in 1779, an "Essai sur l'isle d'Otahiti", which oifers a pleasant jumble of Montesquieu, Rousseau, and Hawkesworth: "Il est doux de penser que la philanthropic semble naturelle à tous les hommes, et que les idées sauvages de défiance et de haine ne sont que la suite de la dépravation de moeurs, qui ne peut exister chez un peuple qui n'en a pas même l'idée."

The naturalist, Commerson, who accompanied Bougainville, was the source of most of the pretty French illusions about Tahiti. His letter, published in the "Mercure de France", in November, 1769, was a romance in the style and in the spirit of Rousseau. It is too long to quote in full, but some of its passages are marvels of literature and science. He began by calling the island Utopia, not then knowing that his chief, Bougainville, had called it New Cytherea:

"Je puis vous dire que c'est le seul coin de la terre où habitent des hommes sans vices, sans préjugés, sans besoins, sans dissensions. Nés sous le plus beau ciel, nourris des fruits d'une terre féconde sans culture, régis par des pères de famille plutôt que par des rois, ils ne connaissent d'autre dieu que l'Amour. Tous les jours lui sont consacrés, toute l'isle est son temple, toutes les femmes en sont, les autels, tous les hommes les sacrificateurs. Et quelles femmes, me demanderez-vous? les rivales des Géorgiennes en beauté et les soeurs des grâces toutes nues."

Omitting his further remarks on this subject, which rose to the dizzy height of affirming that, in Tahiti, "l'acte de créer son semblable est un acte de religion", the next of Gommerson's scientific observations is that "tout chez eux est marqué de la plus parfaite intelligence". Even more admirable than their intelligence was their philanthropy:

"Pour ce qui regarde la simplicité de leurs moeurs, l'honnêteté de leurs procédés, surtout envers leurs femmes, qui ne sont nullement subjuguées chez eux comme chez les sauvages, leur philadelphie entre eux tous, leur horreur pour l'effusion du sang humain, leur respect idolâtre pour leurs morts, qu'ils ne' regardent que comme des gens endormis, leur hospitalité enfin pour les étrangers, il faut laisser aux journaux le mérite de s'étendre sur chacun de ces articles, comme notre admiration et notre reconnaissance le requerrent."

Still more wonderful, "leur aversion pour le vin et les liqueurs était invincible, hommes sages en tout!" That they showed ignorance of European conventions in the matter of property was not their fault, but a virtue:

"Je ne les quitterai pas, ces chers Taïtiens, sans les avoir lavés d'une injure qu'on leur a faite en les traitant de voleurs. Il est vrai qu'ils nous ont enlevé beaucoup de choses, et cela même avec une dextérité qui ferait honneur au plus habile filou de Paris; mais méritent-ils pour cela le nom de voleurs? Voyons ce que c'est que le vol? c'est l'enlèvement d'une chose qui est en propriété à un autre, il faut donc que ce quelqu'un se plaigne justement d'avoir été volé, qu'il lui ai été enlevé un effet sur lequel son droit de propriété était préétabli; mais ce droit de propriété est-il dans la nature? non: il est de pure convention; or, aucune convention n'oblige qu'elle ne soit connue et acceptée. Or, le Taïtien qui n'a rien à lui, qui offre et donne généreusement tout ce qu'il voit désirer, ne l'a jamais connu ce droit exclusif! donc l'acte d'enlèvement qu'il vous a fait d'une chose qui excite sa curiosité, n'est, selon lui, qu'un acte d'équité naturelle... Je ne vois pas l'ombre d'un vol là-dedans."

The natural goodness of the human heart and the moral blessings of a state of nature, were the themes of all Rousseau's followers, and at that time all Europe was following Rousseau. The discovery of Tahiti, as Wallis and Commerson painted it, was the strongest possible proof that Rousseau was right. The society of Tahiti showed that European society had no real support in reason or experience, but should be abolished, with its absurd conventions, contrary to the natural rights and innate virtue of man. The French philosophers seriously used Tahiti for this purpose, and with effect, as every one knows. Wallis's queen played a chief part in the European play, by exciting interest and sympathy; for the years before and after 1770 were sentimental, and, between Diderot's Orou and Goethe's Werter, the sentimental princess of Hawkesworth's voyages was at home. As the queen, according to our family record, was our great-great-grandaunt Purea, or rather the wife of our great-great-granduncle, and as I know something about Tahitian women, and especially about this one by tradition, I will not deny that perhaps Dr. Hawkesworth may have added some color of rose to the story that Wallis had to tell; but this has nothing to do with the curious accident that Tahiti really influenced Europe, and that our great-great-grandaunt, "my princess, or rather, queen", was, without her own knowledge or consent, directly concerned in causing the French Revolution and costing the head of her sister queen, Marie Antoinette.

As Diderot and Commerson show, the interest felt in France for the state of nature in Tahiti was largely caused by the eternal dispute about marriage and the supposed laxity of Tahitian morals in regard to the relations of men and women. I say "supposed" because no one knows how much of the laxity was due to the French and English themselves; whose appearance certainly caused a sudden and shocking overthrow of such moral rules as had existed before in the island society; and the "supposed" means that when the island society as a whole is taken into account, marriage was real as far as it went, and the standard rather higher than that of Paris; in some ways extremely lax, and in others strict and stern to a degree that would have astonished even the most conventional English nobleman, had he understood it. The real code of Tahitian society would have upset the theories of a state of nature as thoroughly as the guillotine did; but, when seen through the eyes of French and English sailors, who had not the smallest sense of responsibility, and would not have been sorry to overthrow all standards, Tahiti seemed to prove that no standard was necessary, which made the island interesting to philosophers and charming to the French people, never easy under even the morality recognized at Paris. So there again our aunt Purea, Wallis's queen, played a part in the drama, for, in an island which seemed to have no idea of morals, she was a model of humanity, sentiment, and conduct -- the flower of a state of nature.

Of course the sentiment of Hawkesworth, and the Gytherean tastes of Bougainville and Commerson, did not please every one, least of all in England, where French philosophy and shepherdesses were rarely welcome. A friend has given me a quotation from Horace Walpole, who wrote to one of his correspondents in 1773: "I hope you are heartily provoked at the new Voyages, which might make one a good first mate, but tell one nothing at all. Dr. Hawkesworth is still more provoking. An old black gentlewoman of forty carries Captain Wallis across a river when he was too weak to walk, and the man represents them as a new edition of Dido and Æneas." Whatever pleased the French was pretty sure to displease the English, and so, from the first, Tahiti took a French color which ended by deciding its fate; and there, too, our aunt Purea unconsciously may have been a chief agent in causing the sentimental attachment which brought the French squadrons seventy years later to our shores.

CHAPTER VII

Wallis left the island in July, 1767. Bougainville visited it in April, 1768, but touched only at Hitiaa, on the eastern side. Amo and Purea were probably then at Papara, preparing for the great feast at which Teriirere i Tooarai was to wear the Maro for the first time in his great new Marae at Mahaiatea.

This feast was the last display of Purea's pride. The contest she had challenged began by a disturbance which broke up the Ahu raa reva -- the donning of the Maro ura -- which was the equivalent of coronation among a people who never wore a crown. The unfortunate Teriirere, for whose sake the feast and the Rahui and the Marae were made, found his cousins uniting to pull him down. The Tevas of Papara have preserved a song made in memory of this tragedy, and almost as lyric and lurid as the tragedy itself; but so genuine a piece of native literature that I have done my best to write it down correctly, and get explanations of its obscure allusions.

The words, with their literal translation, run thus:

AHU RAA REVA. THE FEAST OF TOOARAI

1

Ahu raa reva i Tooarai
Patiri ite pae ote rai
Tu'ua tetapii ite avatea
Haati ite reva ate arii
Te arii ite rai tauatini
Hapuni ite reva ate arii
Te arii ite rai tauamano
E faatia raa reva tei Matahihae
Ite aro o Vehiatua
Na taata i ofati ite reva ate arii
O Teieie raua o Tetumanua
Ahiri toe hara i hope i reira
I ati te Oropaa
Na hia faifai roa te pohe ote fenua
Na hara ,oe ete Purahi
Ite reva ura ate arii

The feast of flags was held at Tooarai
(The drums) like crash of thunder along the sky
(The splendor) like the rays of noonday sun
Surrounded the standard of the arii
The arii of countless skies
Enveloped the standard of the arii
The arii of a thousand skies.
A feast was also held at Matahihae
In the presence of Vehiatua
The two men who broke up the feast of the arii
Were Teieie and Tetumanua
Had the sin ceased there
It brought misery to the Oropaa
And the whole land was laid prostrate

Tei fati hia e Taiarapu
A pohe ai tatou e

Oh, thou hast sinned, Purahi,
Against the reva ura of thine Arii
That was broken up by Taiarapu
Which brought on our ruin.

2

E tatari oe ite nuu nui ite patu ofai
Ite marae i Mahaiatea
Pohuatea tei Punaauia
Tepauarii tei Ahurai
Teriimaroura tei Tarahoi
Te fenua i hara atu ai te maau e
Eimeo ite raravaru
Te fenua i tai hia e Mahine
Na oti ite pure, tootoo ia ite iho na
O Puni i Farerua, o Raa i Tupai
E tahua o Teae afano i Tahiti
E oroa tei Tahiti
Ahu raa reva na Teriirere i Tooarai
Tatou e no ho ai e
Na hara oe ete Purahi
Ite reva ura ate arii
Tei fati hia e Taiarapu
A pohe ai tatou e

Assembles the great host at the cairn
At the marae of Mahaietea.
Pohuatea at Punaauia.
Tepauarii at Ahurai.
Terii maro ura at Tarahoi
The land where the idiot was punished.
Eimeo, the eight branched,
The land dear to Mahine.
The prayers were said, the call was given
To Puni of Farerua, to Raa of Tupai
The high priest Teae is gone to Tahiti
There is a feast at Tahiti
The Ahuraareva for Teriirere of Tooarai
To whom we all bow down.
Oh, thou hast sinned, Purahi,
Against the reva ura of thine Arii
That was broken up by Taiarapu
Which brought on our ruin.

3

Faaara viriaro tei Pafaarava

The scouts at Pafaarava are wakened

E rima tahivai e rima tahivai

Eha ei roto e ha ei rapae

Ahiri ite tao a Amo e

E te Oropaa e

E hopoipoi tia tatou

Ite aro na tai ote vaa

Nauta tatou hoe ona a ino

Tei mua ite Malataupe

E aau paapaa tei Vaitoata

E pau tatou ite pau o Pairituaipo

Ite rahi tauraa Temahuru nia nei

Pahupua ma nei

Hia orero tina Papara

Na hia te moua

Ite vaa nui o Hui ma Taiarapu

Hoe noa tia ei te pae tahatai

Tau mate o no iaia e

Na hara oe ete Purahi

Ite reva ura ate arii

Tei fati hia e Taiarapu

A pohe ai tatou e

One hand is stretched out, and then another.

The four (districts) within, and the four without

Ah, had the advice of Amo been followed

By you of the Oropaa

To lead us all

The van of the army by canoes on the sea

By the mountain-road we had one evil

Ahead of us at the Matataupe

The dry reef of Vaitoata

There we might have died the death of Pairituaipo

At the meeting-ground of Temahuru

And of Pahupua.

Papara is laid prostrate

The Mount (the Arii) is laid low

By the great army of Hui and Taiarapu

Only one now stands on the shore, the Marae,

Thou the cause of our downfall.

Oh, thou hast sinned, Purahi,

Against the reva ura of thine Arii

That was broken up by Taiarapu

Which brought on our ruin.

From this song we can make out that Purahi was the woman who caused the disaster at last. Purahi was an Aromaiterai; the daughter of the Aromaiterai who married Amo's sister Tetuaunurau somewhere about 1750 (See Table I). She was therefore first cousin of the young Teriirere, and belonged to the elder branch of the family, while Teriirere was a Tuiterai, and by his mother, Purea, not a Teva at all. According to island law, I suppose Purahi had a perfect right to take the power from Teriirere if she could.

Purahi was supported by Vehiatua; and the army that devastated Papara came from Taiarapu and Hui. It was led by the great warriors, Teieie and

Tetumanua, who were, and are still, so famous that even today you may hear the Taiarapu sing of them. Teieie was a cousin of Vehiatua, and is our ancestor, which is not the case with Amo. My father Tati was, as Table II shows, the son of Teuraiterai and Telau of Ravea. Tetau was a granddaughter of Teieie.

Only the other day I heard the Tautira people again sing the last verses of the song which told how Vehiatua remonstrated with Teieie for troubling his authority. The first part is forgotten. The verses I heard were these:

VEHIATUA TO TEIEIE

Teieie, e eiaha ei faainoino ite hau

Teieie, why, oh! why will you make trouble with the government!

Tena ta oe ite ra e hiti

You have the sun-rise (the Pari)

I Tirimiro i Manuataha.

The Tirimiro and Manuataha (sub-districts).

TEIEIE TO VEHIATUA

Te mata toana te mata toanei

You have eyes, eyes have I!

Te huru toa nei te huru toa nei

You are a warrior, warrior am I!

Haapiti te matai e nauta mai i Tahuarera

Haapite the wind that blows over Tahuarera

Ite rua o matai taua Fatutira ite tai paaina

Brings me the sound of the surf of Fatutira.

O Murihau a nae ra o tau e tai.

Murihau is all I ask and cry for.

Needless to say that Murihau was another village beauty, like the Maraeura of Tauraatua, whose rank was too low for marriage with an Arii.

Teieie and Tetumanua were called the Ohiteitei -- the two serpents. In honor of them all Taiarapu was called Upoeeha. These two great warriors broke up the Feast of Tooarai, and laid low the Moua, the Arii Teriirere, "in whose presence we all go on our knees".

The various great chiefs who were summoned to the Feast show the extent of Teriirere's influence. Besides Pohuatea at Punaauia, Tepau at Ahurai, and Terii maro ura at Tarahoi, the island of Eimeo was summoned and Puni of Farerua in Borabora, and Raa of Tupai and Maupiti, two islands dependent on Borabora; and finally Teae of Baiatea. A curious bit of old history and manners is preserved in the two lines:

Terii maroura tei Tarahoi Maraianaunau

Te fenua i hara atu ai te maau e.

Idiots were objects of respect in most of the ancient societies, and it seems that a certain Teva idiot must have been an object of great interest, for when he was killed, in the district of Pare, for some offence such as implied that he was considered sane and responsible, the Tevas took up arms and revenged his death by ravaging Pare, and retained the event as a sort of epithet in song against the Porionuu and the Arii of Raianaunau.

The Papara people who made the song seem to have been angry because Amo's advice was not followed in the manner of meeting the invasion. If Captain Cook understood them rightly, they laid their disaster on their neighbor, the Arii of Paea, or Attahuru. Certain it is that, when the blow came, Purea, Amo and Teriirere made their escape across the mountains to Haapape, whose chief was a cousin or uncle of Amo. Purea did not take refuge with her own family. But possibly other reasons controlled their movements, for the song says that the whole Oropaa suffered; and Purea's family district of Ahurai may not have escaped, for Ahurai is but a narrow strip of coast, seven kilometers in length, lying directly next to the Oropaa.

On all these intricate points of island politics, Captain Cook was suddenly thrown, with the effect of confusing and irritating him and all the chiefs he had to deal with. He never quite succeeded in understanding their position or his own. His story is the liveliest picture of our misfortunes.

CHAPTER VIII

On the 13th April, 1769, about two years after Wallis's visit, and four months after the raid against Papara, Captain Cook entered Mata-ai Bay in H. M. bark, the "Endeavor," on his first voyage round the world. He found a chief, whose name he understood to be Tootahah, which would now be spelled Tutaha, exercising the powers of government in the district, and under Tootahah's protection he set up his tents on Point Venus. A staff of scientific gentlemen were with him; among them Joseph Banks, afterwards Sir Joseph, who kept a diary, and Dr. Solander, a Swedish naturalist. Another person seems to have been with them who also kept a diary, which was published anonymously in 1772 as "A Journal of a Voyage round the World."

On the 28th April, a fortnight after their arrival, Banks was at work in a tent on shore, with a number of natives seated about, and looking at his doings, when the ship's master entered.

"After breakfast", Banks wrote in his journal, "Jon Mollineux came ashore, and the moment he entered the tent, fixed his eyes upon a woman who was sitting there, and declared that she had been the queen when the 'Dolphin' was here. She also instantly acknowledged him as a person whom she had seen before. Our attention was now entirely diverted from every other object to the examination of a personage we had heard of so much in Europe; she appeared to be about forty, tall and very lusty, her skin white and her eyes full of meaning; she might have been handsome when young, but now few or no traces of it were left. As soon as her Majesty's quality was known to us, she was invited to go on board the ship, where no presents were spared that were thought to be agreeable to her in consideration of her services to the ' Dolphin'. Among other things a child's doll was given to her, of which she seemed very fond; on her landing she met Hercules (whom for the future I shall call by his real name Dootahah [Tutaha]), and showed him her presents He became uneasy, and was not satisfied till he also had got a doll, which he now seemed to prefer to a hatchet; after this, however, dolls were of no value."

Captain Cook also recorded in his Journal the reappearance of Wallis's queen:

"She first went to Mr Banks's tent at the fort, where she was not known till the master happening to go ashore, who knew her and brought her on board with two men and several women who seemed to be all of her family. I made them all some presents or other, but to Oberiea (for that is this woman's name), I gave several things, in return for which, as soon as I went on shore with her, she gave me a hog and several branches of plaintains These she caused to be carried from her canoes up to the fort in a kind of procession, she and I bringing up the rear. This woman is about forty years of age, and, like most of the other women, very masculine. She is head or chief of her own family or Tribe, but to all appearance hath no authority over the rest of the inhabitants, whatever she might have when the 'Dolphin' was here. Hercules, whose real name is Tootaha, is to all appearance the chief man of the island;... he was with us at this time, and did not appear very well pleased at the notice we took of Oberiea".

From these two Journals, Hawkesworth compiled the "Voyages", the first volume of which so much irritated Horace Walpole. For the sake of showing how much, or how little, was added or altered by Hawkesworth, I will give also the page which he devoted to Oberea's rediscovery.

"Canoes were constantly coming in all this forenoon, and the tents at the fort were crowded with people of both sexes from different parts of the island. I was myself busy on board the ship, but Mr. Mollineux, our master, who was one of those that made the last voyage in the 'Dolphin,' went on shore. As soon as he entered Mr. Banks's tent he fixed his eyes upon one of the women, who was sitting there with great composure among the rest, and immediately declared her to be the person who at that time was supposed to be Queen of the island, she also at the same time acknowledging him to be one of the strangers whom she had seen before. The attention of all present was now directed from every other object, and wholly engaged in considering a person who had made so distinguished a figure in the accounts that had been given of this island by its first discoverers; and we soon learnt that her name was Oberea. She seemed to be about forty years of age, and was not only tall but of a large make; her skin was white, and there was an uncommon intelligence and sensibility in her eyes; she appeared to have been handsome when she was young, but at this time little more than memorials of her beauty were left.

"As soon as her quality was known an offer was made to conduct her to the ship. Of this she readily accepted, and came on board with two men and several women, who seemed to be all of her family; I received her with such marks of distinction as I thought would gratify her most, and was not sparing of my presents, among which this august personage seemed particularly delighted with a child's doll. After some time spent on board I attended her back to the shore, and as soon as we landed she presented me with a hog and several bunches of plantains, which she caused to be carried from her canoes up to the fort in a kind of procession, of which she and myself brought up the rear. In our way to the fort we met Tootahah, who, though not king, appeared to be at this time invested with the sovereign authority; he seemed not to be well pleased with the distinction that was shewed to the lady, and became so jealous when she produced her doll that to propitiate him it was thought proper to compliment him with another. At this time he thought fit to prefer a doll to a hatchet; but this preference arose only from a childish jealousy which could not be soothed but by a gift of exactly the same kind with that which had been presented to Oberea."

Every Englishman in those days took comfort, when wandering over the world, in the faith that kings and queens were a part of the divine system, and that no intelligent race could hold up its head without them. A king or a queen the English must have at Tahiti, and they had already settled that Oberea was a queen. What, then, was Tutaha? On going eastward into the district of Papenoo they were told by the natives that all the hogs and poultry belonged to Tutaha and could not be sold without his permission. "We now began to think that this man was indeed a great prince, for an influence so extensive and absolute could be acquired by no other. And we afterwards found that he administered the government of this part of the island, as sovereign, for a minor whom we never saw all the time that we were upon it." Yet they were again perplexed by the sudden appearance of another man, who was treated by the natives with royal honors, within the very district of Haapape where Tutaha seemed to rule.

Cook's Journal, on June 21, contained the following entry:

"This morning a chief whose name is Oamo, and one we had not seen before came to the Fort. There came with him a Boy about seven Years of Age and a Young Woman of about eighteen or twenty. At the Time of their coming, Obariea and several others were in the fort. They went out to meet them, having first uncovered their Heads and Bodies as low as their Waists; and the same thing was done by all those that were on the outside of the Fort. As we looked upon this as a ceremonial respect, and had not seen it paid to anyone before, we thought that this Oamo must be some extraordinary person, and wondered to see so little notice taken of him after the ceremony was over. The Young woman that came along with him could not be prevailed upon to come into the Fort and the Boy was carried upon a Man's back, altho' he was as able to walk as the Man who carried him. This Lead us to inquire who they were; and we was informed that the Boy was heir apparent to the Sovereignty of the Island, and the Young Woman was his Sister, and as such the respect was paid them which was due to no one else except the Arreedehi, which was not Tutaha, from what we could learn, but some other person who we had not seen, or like to do, for they say that he is no Friend of ours, and therefore will not come near us. The Young Boy above mentioned is son to Oamo by Obariea, but Oamo and Obariea do not at this time live together as Man and Wife, he not being able to endure with her troublesome disposition. I mention this because it shows that seperation in the Marriage state is not unknown to these people."

Thus Cook first made the acquaintance of Amo and Teriirere. Banks took no notice, in his Journal, of the incident; but when Hawkesworth came to compile the "Voyage", he added to the account, given in Cook's Journal, some details and made some changes which may have been derived from Banks or Cook, but which were not improvements, and tended to confuse the whole story. Especially he reduced the young woman's age to sixteen, and though continuing to represent her as Teriirere's sister, he said she was intended for his wife. The passage in Hawkesworth runs as follows:

"On the 21st [June] we were visited at the fort by a chief, called Oamo, whom we had never seen before, and who was treated by the natives with uncommon respect; he brought with him a boy about seven years old, and a young woman about sixteen: the boy was carried upon a man's back, which we considered as a piece of state, for he was as well able to walk as any present. As soon as they were in sight, Oberea and several other natives who were in the fort went out to meet them, having first uncovered their heads and bodies as low as the waist: as they came on, the same ceremony was performed by all the natives who were without the fort.... The chief came into the tent, but no entreaty could prevail upon the young woman to follow him, though she seemed to refuse contrary to her inclination: the natives without were indeed all very solicitous to prevent her; sometimes, when her resolution seemed to fail, almost using force: the boy also they restrained in the same manner; but Dr. Solander, happening to meet him at the gate, took him by the hand and led him in before the people were aware of it; as soon, however, as those that were within saw him they took care to have him sent out. These circumstances having strongly excited our curiosity, we enquired who they were, and were informed that Oamo was the husband of Oberea, though they had been a long time separated by mutual consent, and that the young woman and the boy were their children. We learnt also that the boy, whose name was Terridiri, was heir apparent to the sovereignty of the island, and that his sister was intended for his wife, the marriage being deferred only till he should arrive at a proper age. The sovereign at this time was a son of Whappai, whose name was Otou, and who, as before has been observed, was a minor. Whappai, Oamo, and Tootahah were brothers. Whappai was the eldest, and Oamo the second; so that Whappai having no child but Otou, Terridiri, the son of his next brother Oamo, was heir to the sovereignty."

Tahitian genealogy at best was hard to understand, but Captain Cook's struggles with it, aided by English rules, were almost pathetic. On one point he was right. Oamo was Oberea's husband and our great-great-granduncle. Whappai or Hapai is commonly known as Teu, and his son, then called Otoo, was afterward known as Pomare and Vairatoa. As for the relationship of Hapai, Amo and Tutaha, as I have shown, it was not that of brothers. All foreign visitors to Tahiti were misled at first by the Tahitian expressions which meant indifferently brothers and cousins to an indefinite degree. Purea and Otoo were closely connected, as I mean to explain presently, and that Cook should have been confused about the relative rank of Teriirere and Otoo was natural, because at that instant the natives themselves had not decided the question.

The Englishmen soon learned more about the story of Amo and Purea for they set out, only five days after this visit, on a tour round the island, and on June 29th, arrived at Papara, after having made the circuit of Taiarapu. Both Cook and Banks, in their Journals, gave accounts of what they saw there, and from these Hawkesworth made up the description which is published in the "Voyage."

"We were now [June 29] not far from the district called PAPARRA, which belonged to our friends Oamo and Oberea, where we proposed to sleep. We went on shore about an hour before night, and found that they were both absent, having left their habitations to pay us a visit at Matavai: this however, did not alter our purpose; we took up our quarters at the house of Oberea, which, though small, was very neat, and at this time had no inhabitant but her father, who received us with looks that bid us welcome. Having taken possession we were willing to improve the little daylight that was left us, and therefore walked out to a point upon which we had seen, at a distance, trees that are here called Etoa, which generally distinguish the places where these people bury the bones of their dead; their name for such burying grounds, which are also places of worship, is Morai. We were soon struck with the sight of an enormous pile, which we were told was the Morai of Oamo and Oberea, and the principal piece of Indian architecture in the island. It was a pile of stone-work raised pyramidically upon an oblong base or square two hundred and sixty-seven feet long and eighty-seven wide. It was built like the small pyramidal mounds upon which we sometimes fix the pillar of a sun-dial, where each side is a flight of steps; the steps, however, at the sides were broader than those at the ends, so that it terminated not in a square of the same figure with the base, but in a ridge like the roof of a house; there were eleven of these steps, each of which was four feet high, so that the height of the pile was forty-four feet: each step was formed of one course of white coral stone which was neatly squared and polished; the rest of the mass, for there was no hollow within, consisted of round pebbles, which, from the regularity of their figure, seemed to have been wrought. Some of the coral stones were very large; we measured one of them and found it three feet and an half by two feet and an half. The foundation was of rock stones, which were also squared, and one of them measured four feet seven inches by two feet four. Such a structure, raised without the assistance of iron tools to shape the stones or mortar to join them, struck us with atonishment; it seemed to be as compact and firm as it could have been made by any workman in Europe, except that the steps, which range along its greatest length, are not perfectly straight, but sink in a kind of hollow in the middle, so that the whole surface, from end to end, is not a right line but a curve. The quarry stones, as we saw no quarry in the neighborhood, must have been brought from a considerable distance, and there is no method of conveyance here but by hand; the coral must also have been fished from under the water, where, though it may be found in plenty, it lies at a considerable depth, never less than three feet. Both the rock stone and the coral could be squared only by tools made of the same substance, which must have been a work of incredible labor; but the polishing was more easily effected by means of the sharp coral sand which is found everywhere upon the seashore in great abundance. In the middle of the top stood the image of a bird carved in wood, and near it lay the broken one of a fish carved in stone. The whole of this pyramid made part of one side of a spacious area or square, nearly of equal sides, being three hundred and sixty feet by three hundred and fifty-four, which was walled in with stone, and paved with flat stones in its whole extent."

In this instance Hakesworth did not exaggerate the language used by his authorities. Banks used even stronger expressions. "A most enormous pile," he called the Marae; "its size and workmanship almost exceed belief." His measurement differed from that of Cook in regard to breadth. Cook made the base 267 by 87 feet. Banks made it 267 by 71 feet. Cook added that "at the top it is 250 feet by 8 feet." They agreed as to the number of steps but not precisely about their height. "Each step", said Cook, "is about 4 feet in height, and the breadth 4 feet 7 inches, but they decreased both in height and breadth from the bottom to the top."

Only a great heap of shapeless coral stones now remains of the Marae of Mahaiatea, which has been used as a quarry for nearly a century, so that we cannot tell how exact Cook's report was, but both he and Banks were as a rule so accurate and so matter-of-fact that one feels safe in accepting all they said. Nearly thirty years afterward, when the missionaries came in the ship "Duff," they not only took measurements but made a sketch which is engraved in their narrative, and shows the pyramid still almost perfect. They found its length to be two hundred and seventy feet, or three feet more than Cook made it, and its width ninety-four feet, which is seven feet in excess of Cook's measurement. According to their account and the sketch, the pyramid had not eleven but ten steps, the lowest six feet and the other nine about five feet high, which gives a total height of about fifty feet, instead of forty-four. Even in Egypt such a pile would have taken a respectable, place among the small pyramids, but in the South Seas, where continuous labor was hardly possible to obtain or to enforce, and where stone architecture was uncommon, such a monument excited as much astonishment as the famous stone figures of Easter Island or the ruins in Central America would have done.

The Marae of Mahaiatea, which the books so often mention as the Marae of Amo and Purae, not only cost our family a crown, but also very nearly its existence. Banks's narrative grows in interest as it goes on, and the next paragraph comes painfully near us.

"About a hundred yards to the west of this building was another court or paved area, in which were several Ewhattas, a kind of altar raised on wooden pillars about seven feet high; on these they offer meat of all kinds to the gods. We have thus seen large hogs offered; and here were the skulls of about fifty of them, besides those of dogs which the priest who accompanied us assured us were only a small fraction of what had been here sacrificed. This Marai [Tooarai] and apparatus for sacrifice belonged, we were told, to Oborea and Oamo. The greatest pride of an inhabitant of Otaheite is to have a grand Marai; in this particular our friends far exceed any one in the island, and in the Dolphin's time the first of them exceeded everyone else in riches and respect. The reason of the difference of her present appearance I found by an accident which I now relate. Our road to the Marai lay by the seaside, and everywhere under our feet were numberless human bones, chiefly ribs and vertebrae. So singular a sight surprised me much, and I inquired the reason. I was told that in the month called by them Owaraheu last, which answers to our December, 1768, the people of Tiarreboo made a descent here and killed a large number of people whose bones we now saw; that upon this occasion Oborea and Oamo were obliged to flee for shelter to the mountains; that the conquerors burnt all the houses, which were very large, and took away all the hogs, etc; that the turkey and goose which we had seen [in Taiarapu] were part of the spoils, as were the jaw-bones which we had also seen."

Thanks to Banks's exactness, we know, then, that the authority of Amo and Purea, or al least their military domination, was broken down by a sudden attack from Tiarapu in December, 1768, eighteen months after Wallis saw Purea in the pride of her queenship, at Matavai Bay. This gives one of the two certain dates in our family history. The destruction of Papara by the Tiarapu people in December, 1768, was the first of a long series of disasters and miseries which ended with the death of our granduncle Opuhara, at the battle of the Fei-pi, November 12, 1815.

Besides this light thrown on our personal affairs, Cook's first voyage gives another gleam. When Wallis visited the island he found a certain man named Tupia, or Tupaia of Raiatea, high in power and a chief adviser of Purea. When Cook arrived, Tupaia was still there:

"Among the natives who were almost constantly with us was Tupia, whose name has been often mentioned in this narrative. He had been, as I have before observed, the first minister of Oberea when she was in the height of her power; he was also the chief Tahowa or priest of the island; consequently well acquainted with the religion of the country as well with respect to its ceremonies as principles. This man had often expressed a desire to go with us, and on the 12th [July], in the morning, having with the other natives left us the day before, he came on board with a boy about thirteen years of age, his servant, and urged us to let him proceed with us on our voyage."

Cook consented, and Tupaia left the island with him. They arrived at Raiatea, called Ulietea by Cook, on the 20th July, and there, according to the anonymous "Journal," Tupaia gave them some account of himself, which interests us more than it did Cook. He said that he was a native of Raiatea, and had been driven out of it by an invasion and conquest of the island from the little neighboring island of Bora-bora. Having fled to Tahiti he was taken into favor by Purea, and roused the enmity of Tutaha, "uncle to the young king, her son, and a man of great courage, and highly esteemed by the people," but who meditated a change in the regency:

"The better to effect it he began to create divisions between the inhabitants of Otahitee-eta (Taiarapu) and of Otahitee-nua [little Tahiti and big Tahiti], which finally produced hostilities between them. At that time Tobia [Tupaia], who had great sagacity and judgment, having discovered Tutahau's designs, advised the queen to procure his death privately, as the only expedient to restore peace and preserve her authority; but she, thinking his advice too cruel, refused, for the first time, to comply with it; and he, foreseeing the consequences, retired to the mountains, alleging that this retreat was necessary for the preservation of his life. Soon after, the inhabitants of Lesser Otahitee making frequent incursions into the greater division, and their numerous depredations having thrown the inhabitants of the latter into confusion, which Tutahaw artfully improving to his advantage, they at length offered him the regency, thinking their affairs too much embarrassed for the administration of a female; an agreement was therefore made between Oberea and Tutahaw, in which it was conditioned that she should preserve the title and state of queen, with a certain number of attendants, &c., and that the regency should devolve to Tutahaw; who, respecting Tobia's understanding and sacerdotal character, afterward permitted him to return from the mountains in safety; but he was so much displeased with this revolution that he embraced the opportunity of our departure to leave the island."

This account was accepted by George Forster, who accompanied Cook as naturalist in attendance on his father, John Reinold Forster, in 1774, when Cook made his second visit to the island. Forster heard the same story from Otoo's people at Pare Arue. Amo and Purea, in December, 1768, had been driven from Papara into the mountains. "At last the conqueror [Vehiatua] consented to a peace on condition that Amo should entirely resign the government, and that the succession should be taken from his son and conferred upon Otoo, the eldest son of his [Amo's] brother Happai. This was agreed to, and Tootahah, the youngest brother of Amo, was appointed regent." The whole story was bodily adopted thirty years afterward into the Missionary Narrative, but the missionaries added some interesting details not given in the "Journal."

"Waheadooa [Vehiatua of Taiarapu], stimulated by the desire of becoming wholly independent of the larger peninsula, passed the isthmus with his army, and defeated that which Oammo had collected to oppose him. Tootaha, at the same time, with the forces of Attahooroo and Tettaha, attacked from the westward the district of Pappara, Oammo's residence, and carried off from the great morae at that place, to another in Attahooroo, the peculiar ensigns of the regal and sacerdotal offices. The grand ceremonies which are attended with human sacrifices were therefore performed at the morae of Attahooroo for thirteen years after that event. "

These stories seem to show that in December, 1768, the peninsula of Taiarapu in the south, Pare Arue in the north, and the Oro-paa or Paea on the west, combined to attack Papara from both sides and succeeded in crushing it. Vehiatua and the Taiarapu army came from the south and ravaged Papara, after defeating Amo and massacring the people. The human bones still covering the beach in June, 1769, proved the severity of the disaster, and the Taiarapu people showed Cook as trophies, in a single village far down at the extreme corner of their peninsula, fifteen human jaw-bones, perfectly fresh and none of them wanting a single tooth. At the same village Cook saw a goose and a turkey-cock which had been given to Purea by Wallis in 1767, and had become a part of the plunder of Papara. While the Taiarapu people carried off the heads and the property of the victims, Tutaha and the northwestern districts carried away the symbol of supremacy, the standard and feathered girdle, from the Marae of Tooarai and Mahaiatea, and placed it in the Marae of Maraetaata in the district of Paea in the Oropaa, or, as it was usually called by the English, Attahuru. Amo and Purea were forced to make what terms they could with Tutaha, and to recognize Otoo, as having a right to the dignity of the Maro-ura at Maraetata. Papara lost her political supremacy. The coalition of Ahu-rai and Pare Arue with Taiarapu made a new centre of power; but Teriirere remained chief of the Teva districts, retained his social position and the Maro-tea, and was still the most powerful single chief in the island. No one seems to have tried to drive the Papara family out, as Vehiatua drove out Tavi and as Pomare was driven out in 1808. The quarrel was with Purea rather than with Amo or Teriirere.

Tradition further says that Otoo was not allowed to wear the Maro without a protest. In order to receive full recognition, he was obliged to take a seat and wear the Maro-ura in the great Marae of Maraetaata in Paea. This Marae had three heads: (1) Pouira, the Tevahitua i Patea; (2) Tetooha, the Taura atua i Patea; and (3) Punuaaitua. Tevahitua protested, and refused to allow Otoo to take his seat and wear the Maroura on his part of the Marae. The other two made no objection, and the reason was characteristic of Tahitian society. Otoo's great-grandmother, Te-fete-fete-ui, was the daughter of Tevarua hoiatua, a chiefess of Ahurai and Punaauia, and as such had the right to a seat in Marae Maraetaata.

CHAPTER IX

Now that I have told the story of the Papara family and its connections down to the time of the Rahui war of 1768, and the recognition of Otoo's right to wear the Maro-ura at Marae Maraetaata, which happened to coincide with Captain Cook's Voyage, I must take up the story of the Pare Arue family, who under the name of Pomare were to rouse singular interest and passion, not only in Tahiti, but even throughout the Christian world, which became at times, for religious or political reasons, keenly excited about our small island.

Otoo was of course an English name. The full name was Tu-nui-ea-i-te-atu, shortened in common use to the first syllable, Tu, which meant God, whether in its simple monosyllabic form, or in Atua, Aitu and so on. Tu meant the same in most languages, even in English, as in the identical word in Tuesday. I get this information from no deeper source than the Century Dictionary, and claim no credit for it, except that to a European it may help to bring Otoo a little nearer; but whether Tu is English or not, in Tahitian Tu-nui meant a Great God, and the word Tu was a sacred word. I suppose that Tu-i-te-rai is another example of the same thing: God-of-the-Sky. I suppose, too, that Toa, warrior, is a different word, and goes with Duke, and the old Anglo-Saxon here-toga, army-leader; but I mention this only to keep the two ideas separate in the mind of any reader. Tu was a god; Tunui was a great god; and as every chiefly family traced descent from Taaroa or Oro or some of the established deities, the family whose chief bore the title Tunuieaite-atua merely went with the custom of chiefs.

In ordinary native use, the name was simply Tu, the prefix O being no part of the word. I shall, therefore, call him Tu, but to distinguish the succession of Tus, one has to use the other names which the chief had or took. Before touching the family at all, I shall have, also, to make a long digression in regard to the district of Pare and its history, for the Tu family did not originally belong there in the male line and had a wholly different source.

Many Ariis ruled over Pare before the Tu dynasty was known there, and have left legends enough to fill a volume of their own. The names of five were: (1) Tauaitaata; (2) Teuira arii i Ahutoru; (3) Niuhi; (4) Te huritaua o te Mauu; (5) Taihia. Tauaitaata was the subject of a legend or story that shows what the Tahitians thought interesting or so exceptional as to be worth remembering in their own character and society.

Taua-i-taata, or Tau, for short, Arii of Pare, married Taia, sister of Vanaama-i-terai, chief or Arii of Papenoo, the district beyond Haapape, some fourteen or fifteen miles to the east of Pare. They had two children, whose descendants, by the way, remain Arii of Papenoo down to the present day. That they are Arii of Papenoo and not of Pare was due to the feud told in the following legend.

Vanaa of Papenoo had two jesters, a class of men much petted and allowed many liberties by all Arii. Among other privileges, they were always in the habit of receiving some of the best shares in distributions of food by the Arii. Vanaa's two jesters were or thought themselves slighted in some such distribution and swore revenge. They asked permission to visit Tau at Pare, and on their arrival were received by Tau with the usual feast, for which fatted pigs were killed as an offering (Faaamua). When it was brought before them they turned to Tau and thanked him, remarking, with a laugh, that Vanaa had compared him with a pig. Of all the stock insults that are most resented throughout Polynesia, one of the worst is to call a man a pig. Such a man is, like a pig, fit only for sacrifice. Many a death and not a few wars have sprung from this word puaa. Naturally Tau felt himself mortally insulted by his brother-in-law, and lost no time in preparing his revenge.

Ordering a great feast to be made ready at the Marae of Raianaunau, Tau immediately bade his men bring out his canoes, while the two jesters, fearing the consequences of their act, especially to themselves, escaped to Papenoo. Tau's wife, Taia, noticing the preparations, asked her husband where he was going, and he merely replied, "I go to visit your brother." Very little time was needed for expeditions of this sort in the South Seas, unless some ceremony was to be performed or resistance was expected. A few hours would be enough for the insult, the passion, and the revenge. Tau started immediately, and his men soon paddled his canoes round the point at Matavai and abreast of the village of Papenoo, where they stopped and hailed, with the cry that it was Tauaitaata of Pare. The people of Papenoo gathered on the beach to receive him, but were surprised to find that no one came ashore. The Arii himself, Vanaamaiterai, then hailed the canoes and asked, "Why does not Tauaitaata land?" The reply came that the sea was, for the moment, too rough. Then Vanaa, in the courtesy of the chiefly relation, did what Tau intended him to do, he swam out, and on swimming alongside Tau's canoe he was quietly and instantly clubbed on the head and his body drawn into the canoe without betraying to the people on the shore a sign of what was happening. They were only somewhat surprised to see that after their chief had got aboard, alone, the canoes turned and paddled back toward Pare with Vanaa, but without a single attendant.

On arriving at Pare, Tau had the body of Vanaa carried to the Marae of Raianaunau, and without going to his house, followed the body to the Marae where the feast was already prepared. Of course Tau meant that the murder should be kept a secret from his wife until he should be ready to deal with her; but when the drums of the feast began beating for the dead, Taia, hearing them and not hearing of her husband's return, asked: "Why are the drums of Raianaunau beaten?" Her women answered that the Arii must have arrived; but she knew the tones of the pahu too well to be deceived. She listened again, and cried: "That is not for an Arii's arrival; it is for an Arii dead! Who is dead ? Not Tau, for I should have been told! Why am I not told?" She sent one of her women to ask, but the woman came back without an answer. Then Taia sent for her husband, Tau, who sent back word that he could not see her for three days, as his duties or ceremonies required.

This was enough to waken Taia's suspicions. She knew that Tau had abruptly started to visit her brother, and had returned without coming near her, and was making a feast over a dead Arii. She ordered one of her women to go out and look for the first person coming from Papenoo, to ask about Vanaa. Two days passed before the woman reported that she had just seen a man from Papenoo who told her that Vanaa had gone away with Tau, on his return to Pare. "I know now," she cried, "that my brother is dead;" and she ordered the man to be brought to her, to tell her all he could. Then she sent him back instantly to tell the people of Papenoo that their Arii was murdered, and they must send canoes immediately to rescue her. The same evening the boats arrived and she set out in them, taking with her, after much hesitation, her two children.

Then began the part of her activity which was most characteristic of the island society. Custom prescribed a regular course for women who sought justice or revenge. In the murder of Vanaa, Tau had outraged not only the district of Papenoo, of which Vanaa was Arii, but all the districts and Arii connected by political or social ties with Papenoo. The whole eastern coast of Tahiti beyond Pare Arue (Haapape, Papenoo, Tiarei, Mahaena, Hitiaa) formed one connected group known as Teaharoa. When united, the Aharoa were much stronger than the Purionuu, or Pare Arue, where Tau was Arii. To revenge her brother, Taia had to visit each of the Aharoa Arii in turn, and claim his assistance, which, in such cases, was seldom refused.

Accordingly Taia stopped first at Haapape and made her complaint. Then, continuing on her way eastward, she stopped abreast of her landing-place at Papenoo, where the beach was already crowded with people awaiting her; but she cried out: "I will not land! My orders are: Let no one pass through Papenoo! Bind the two jesters! Prepare for war! Wait my return! I go to tie our alliance of the six Teaharoas!" Going directly on to Tiarei and Mahaena, she ended her journey at Hitiaa, received everywhere with open arms and pledges of support. Returning to Papenoo, she put the two jesters to death and their bodies were taken to the Marae. This done, she waited the arrival of the other districts to make the attack on Pare.

Against such an attack the chief of Pare seems to have felt himself helpless, for when his feast was over, and he learned that his wife and children had fled, he knew what she would do to revenge her brother, and, without waiting for the invasion from Teaharoa, he escaped to Moorea.

With his departure, his line ceased to be Arii of Pare. He never appeared there again. His wife, afterward married Tevahitua i Patea, and from this marriage our Papara family is descended,

Tau was followed in Pare by Teuira-arii, of whom little is remembered except that he was beaten in battle, and as usual lost his chiefery.

Then came Niuhi, who was the subject of another tragedy caused by his killing the two sons of a man named Tetohu of Faaa, and placing their bodies on the Marae of Raianaunau. When the father heard of their death he called his daughter Terero and said to her: "I have just heard that my sons are put to death by Niuhi, and I am going to Raianaunau to mourn for them." She remonstrated: "Do not go! You will be killed." "I will go!" he replied; "but I wish you to wait three days, and if I do not return I shall be dead. Then go to Hitiaa, where you will find Teriimana, Arii of Moorea, who is feasting withTeriitua at Hitiaa. Say to him that I, Tetohu, beg him to revenge the death of my sons. The Fee [cuttle-fish or squid] has eight tentacles. Temahue, the mount of Pare, has eight peaks. There are eight districts of Moorea. There still remain the head and two eyes of the Fee. Give the head to Tefana i Ahurai: one eye to Teruru of Pereaitu (of Paea); the other eye to Vavahiiteraa (of Mahaena). If Terimana accepts my request, beg him to leave instantly for Moorea, start the war-canoes, and give battle to the Arii Niuhi."

The figure of the cuttle-fish was very characteristic of Tahitian ways of talking, which seemed to find metaphor necessary for intelligent expression. The head and two eyes of the squid were Niuhi and his two sons. The eight tentacles were the eight districts of the Purionuu.

After giving these instructions to his daughter, Tetohu bade her farewell and started for Marae Raianaunau, where he arrived the same evening, and found the bodies of his sons on the Marae, tied together and covered with a cloth of tapa. He uncovered and separated them, and then lay down between them, with their heads on his arms, and there he lay till, in the morning, the Tahua or priest, coming to the Marae to prepare the sacrifice, was surprised to see six legs instead of four under the tapa covering. Lifting it, he saw Tetohu, and was so deeply touched by his mournful face, with the dead sons lying in his arms, that he had not the heart to call the alarm, which must be the signal for the death of the father. "Get up and fly while there is yet time," he said to Tetohu. "Do you not know that it is death to interfere with Niuhi's vengeance and mount his Marae of Raianaunau?" Tetohu answered: "I have come to follow the fate of my sons, sure that my revenge is close at hand." The Tahua had then no choice for his own life but to report the event to Niuhi, who instantly ordered Tetohu to be killed.

The daughter waited till the third day passed without her father's return, and then, knowing he was dead, she hurried to Hitiaa. Throwing herself before Teriimana or Temana, she said: "I have come to ask you to revenge the death of my father and brothers." "Against whom?" asked Temana. "Against Niuhi, Arii of Pare." Temana asked for what reason they had been killed. "That is a mystery," she replied.

This habit, that any one with a grievance could appeal before another Arii, made public law in Tahiti. Ariis rarely refused to take up such a quarrel, and sometimes, as I shall have occasion to show from our own family, risked their whole fortune to do it. Temana replied to Terero by the usual formula, bidding her go home, he would attend to her complaint. She then repeated to him her father's message, which he heard with close attention and instantly obeyed. Calling out his followers, he prepared at once to start, and on arriving at Nuurua in Moorea he sent messengers to Namiro of Tefana i Ahurai, to Teruru of Pereaitu, and to Tevavahiiteraa of Mahaena for their help. They accepted, and their acceptance insured the downfall of Niuhi, for they completely surrounded him and cut off all hope of succor or escape. The war-canoes attacked by sea under Temana; on the Faaa side Namiro and Teruru led Ahurai to the attack by land; on the Mahaena side Tevavahiteraa closed the path. Niuhi was surprised, captured, and bound.

Another curious custom of war was shown in this affair of Niuhi, who seems to have been the object of rather unusual hatred. Temana, having led the attack, was perhaps required by courtesy to share his victim with his allies. He invited them to exercise the right of offering the worst insult that could be inflicted on an Arii, of beating the back of the victim with their spears, as he lay bound. Namiro, who figured as the head of the cuttle-fish, was the first to strike. "I am a prisoner," said Niuhi, who could not see, and did not know his captors; "I am dishonored by any one who strikes me on the back; but still I have the right to ask who strikes me." "I am Namiro, the warrior of Ahurai," was the answer; "I beat you with my lance Tuahinearama-rama." Niuhi was silent. Teruru of Pereaitu stepped forward next and struck. Niuhi repeated his question, and was told: "I am Teruru of Pereaitu. I strike you with my lance Teaho." Again Niuhi was silent. Tevavahiiteraa struck next. "Who is that?" asked Niuhi; "what wood is your lance made of?" "It is the apiri of Tamahue,' replied Tevava, with another insult, for the apiri is only a weed. "No!" said Niuhi; "the apiri would sting, and would make a singing in the air as it struck, while this falls on my back with a dull thud." "Know, then!" said Vavahiiteraa, "that it is the Teae of Mouoe!" The teae was a hard wood growing only on the hills of Mahaena. "I know now that I am lost," said Niuhi, "for I am surrounded."

Niuhi lost his chiefery, indeed, but he is supposed to have escaped to the mountains, for he was afterwards again heard of and killed at Papara. Among the fragments of history that survive in the island is a song called the "Boast of Niufi," or Niuhi, which is, as usual, so crowded with local allusions as to be unintelligible, but which seems to show that in his day he was a powerful chief, who ruled over the Aharoa districts as well as the Purionuu. I quote a few lines only to show its form:

THE BOAST OF NIUFI

E fatu rau i tau hau o Taveroiterai

I te talua o Manavataia. te tootoo o Ninihotetoa.

Te taamu o Tiaperetii. te tahiri o Nunaaehau.

E too rau i tau nuu Pare Arue Mahine

Teharuru Eue Temehiti Ahuare Tetaero.

To ina te horo i paepae iriiri e maau rau nei na Teva.

"I am lord of my chiefdom of Taveroiterai

Of the girdle of Manavataia, the staff of Niniho-te-toa,

The union of Tiaperetii, the fan of Nunaaehau.

I am leader of my armies: Pare, Arue, Mahine,

Te Haururu, Eue, Temehiti, Ahuare, Tetaero.

Ask the fall of Paepae-iriiri if I am the idiot of Teva!"

Although the idiot of Teva again appears here, Niufi and his boast now concern our side of the island very little and the Pomares not at all, for in Niufi's time the ancestors of the Pomares were still probably chiefs of Fakarava or Faarava, one of the low coral islands of the Pau-motu archipelago, some two hundred and fifty miles northeast of Tahiti. The exact date of the first Tu's arrival in Tahiti is unknown. Even the generation cannot be fixed. I can say with certainty only that the Pomares were always ashamed of their Paumotu descent, which they considered a flaw in their heraldry and which was a reproach to them in the eyes of Tahitians, for all Tahitians regarded the Paumotus as savage and socially inferior. The Pomares religiously tried to hide the connection in every possible way, and very few Tahitians would have dared to make even an allusion to the subject in their presence, for it might have been taken as an insult and perhaps cost the jester his life. Once such an allusion was tried and was ignored. Moe, the wife of Tama-toa, son of Pomare IV, and herself Queen of Raiatea, was talking with her mother-in-law, Queen Pomare IV -- Aimata, of whom I shall have much to say, -- who spoke of naming one of her horses "Teva." Moe objected that Teva was a name to which the Pomares had no right; "It belongs to me, the great-grandchild of Tati. Why don't you call your horse 'Paumotu'?" The queen quietly replied: "That's an idea! My father was very fond of the Paumotus. I remember when they came to visit Tahiti, Pomare used to receive them as his most honored guests, and I was often the loser by it."

Aimata's son, Pomare V, the last king, wanting to establish his title to lands in the Paumotus, had naturally to acknowledge the connection and to prove his descent. The genealogy adopted for the occasion made the first Tu, who came from the Paumotus, grandfather to Taaroa manahune, who married Tetuaehuri i Taiarapu, as I have told in Chapter III. Tu of Faarava, having undertaken a visit to the distant land of Tahiti, came in by the Taunoa opening, which is the eastern channel into what is now the harbor of Papeete. Landing at Taunoa a stranger, he was invited to be the guest of Mauaihiti, who seems to have been a chief of Pare. Tu made himself so agreeable, or so useful to his host, that Mauaihiti adopted him as hoa, or brother, with the formal ceremonies attached to this custom, which consist in a grand feast, and union of all the families, and offering of all the rights and honors which belong to the host. Tu accepted them, and at the death of Mauaihiti he became heir and successor in the chiefs line. He gave up all idea of returning to the Paumotus, and devoted his energy to extending his connections in Tahiti. He himself married into the Arue family, which gave his son a claim to the joint chiefery of Pare Arue; and at last his grandson, or some later generation, obtained in marriage no less a personage than Tetuaehuri, daughter of Vehiatua of Taiarapu. The received genealogy represents the son of Taaroa manahune and Tetuaehuri as Teu, who was known as Hapai or Whappai to the English, and lived into this century, but Tahitian genealogies have a perplexing way of dropping persons who do not amuse them, and there may well be a leap of one or two generations in that of Pomare.

I have already said that, according to our Teva genealogies, at least two generations should have lived between Taaroa manahune and Teu, but, however this may be, Teu was born about 1720, and married first Tetupaiai Hauiri, of the head-chiefs of Raiatea. This was another step upward in the social scale. Raiatea and Rorabora, which belong to the group of high islands about one hundred and thirty miles northwest of Tahiti, had head-chiefs of their own, who wore the Maro-ura in their own Marae, and had their great Mouas, Tahuas, and Outus which took rank with, or above, the oldest of Tahiti. In the hierarchy of the Tahitian society, Tetupaia gave to her descendants the claim to wear the Maro-ura in Raiatea.

E Moua inia o Teaetapu

E Tahua o Hauiri

E Outu o Matahira-i-terai

E Marae o Taputapuatea.

The son of Tetupaia and Teu had not only the right to a seat in the great Marae of Taputapuatea in Raiatea, but he could take his stone from Taputapuatea and set it up in his own district of Pare Arue, so founding a Marae Taputapuatea of his own to wear the Maro-ura in. This he did. Some of Vancouver's officers at Matavai, in 1792, "embarked in a canoe belonging to Mowree, the sovereign of Ulietea [Raiatea], who, together with Whytooa [Vaetua] and his wife, accompanied them [from Matavai] toward Oparre [Pare]. On their way they landed for the purpose of seeing the Morai of Tapootapootatea." This must have been at or near Tarahoi, and Tu wore the Maro-ura there in his right ot descent from Raiatea before he was ever permitted to wear it at Maraetaata.

CHAPTER X

Thus, when the Papara family, under the control of Purea, committed the follies which ended in the grand disaster of December, 1768, the Pare Arue family was able to profit by what ruined us. Old Teu, or Hapai, seems to have been a shrewd and cautious man, but we know little about him before Cook arrived. He never assumed to be a great chief or to wear the Maro-ura, and is more likely to have been jealous of his son than of Amo or Teriirere. This son, Tu, must have been born about 1743. From his mother he had a claim to the Maro-ura of Raiatea; through his ancestress Tetuaehuri he belonged to the family of Vehiatua and the Tevaitai districts of Taiarapu; from his father he inherited the chiefery of Pare Arue, and to complete the circle of ambition, he was given a wife -- Tetuanui-rea-i-te-rai -- of the adjoining, independent, chiefery of Tefana i Ahurai, who was not only niece of Purea, but was quite as ambitious and energetic as Purea herself.

I have already told the story of Purea's downfall, as it was told to Cook. According to that account, the chief who accomplished the overthrow of Papara was Tutaha of Paea, and, in fact, whenever Papara has been worsted it has generally been found that Paea helped to turn the scale. Tutaha seems to have taken the lion's share in the division of spoils. Tu got little or nothing except the recognition of his right to wear the Maro-ura at Maraetaata. Further than this his supremacy did not go. Outside his own personal territory he was still a stranger. Although he was recognized by his family and by Tutaha of Paea as an Arii rahi with the Maro-ura in December, 1768, or January, 1769, yet when Cook arrived at Matavai in the following April he never saw Tu; he saw only Tutaha. When he sent a boat along the coast to the eastward, past Papenoo and Mahaena, twenty miles, the people everywhere said that the pigs and other provisions all belonged to Tutaha, and could not be sold without his permission; so that "we now began to think that this man was indeed a great prince, for an influence so extensive and absolute could be acquired by no other; and we afterwards found that he administered the government of this part of the island, as sovereign, for a minor whom we never saw all the time that we were upon it." Although Tu was not a minor, being then fully twenty-five years old, and married; and although he and his wife Tetua must have been burning with curiosity to see Cook and get presents, they could not come to Matavai because Matavai was in the district of Haapape, and they were obliged to look at Cook's ships from a distance, and allow Tutaha and Tepau-i-Ahurai Tamaiti (Toubourai Taimaide) to beg all Cook's axes and nails.

On the other hand, Amo and Purea, although only three or four months had passed since their overthrow, came to Matavai to see Cook, and were received with the usual respect due to Arii rahi. I have already quoted the story, and will quote it again. "On the 21st [June, 1769]," Cook reported "we were visited at the fort by a chief called Oamo, whom we had never seen before, and who was treated by the natives with uncommon respect; he brought with him a boy about seven years old, and a young woman about sixteen: the boy was carried upon a man's back, which we considered as a piece of state, for he was as well able to walk as any present. As soon as they were in sight, Oberea and several other natives who were in the fort went out to meet them, having first uncovered their heads and bodies as low as the waist; as they came on, the same ceremony was performed by all the natives who were without the fort." The boy, Teriirere of Papara, was Arii rahi in Haapape because his father's mother, Tiipaarii or Teroroeora i Fareroi, was a daughter of the chief of Haapape, and Teriirere had a seat in the Marae of Faroroi. Tu had no seat there, and no rights; at that time he did not even dare to enter the district, or come in his canoe into Matavai Bay.

The coalition against Papara fell to pieces as quickly as it was made. Tutaha quarreled with Vehiatua, we know not for what reason, and undertook to break down the Outer Tevas as he had broken down the Inner Tevas. Such a scheme could not have been in the interest of Tu, who owed most of his power to his alliance with Vehiatua; and the plan was openly opposed by old Teu, or Hapai, Tu's father, but without effect. Tu was obliged to follow Tutaha. I will quote what we know of the story, from the missionaries' sketch of island history in the "Voyage of the Duff," taken almost wholly from Forster.

"Tootaha had obtained a great quantity of curious and useful articles from his European guests, and he availed himself of the acquisitions to increase his influence over the chiefs of the larger peninsula. He succeeded in persuading them to unite their forces against Teiar-raboo, which he wished to reduce to its former state of subjection. Waheadooa, who fought only to enjoy peaceably the independence he had established, pleaded the services he had rendered to Tootaha as an argument to divert him from his hostile designs, which Waheadooa had learned and was prepared to resist. The military pride and ambition of the regent urged him to persist in his attempt; and having equipped a fleet of war-canoes, he sailed toward the smaller peninsula and engaged the naval force of Waheadooa, with nearly equal loss on each side. Tootaha retired, with a determination to try his success by land. His brother Happae disapproved of this measure and remained at Oparre; but Tootaha obliged Otoo, who always disliked fighting, to accompany the army. It engaged that of Waheadooa at the isthmus and was totally routed. Tootaha and Tooboorae Tamaede were killed on the spot, Orette [chief of Hitiaa] and many others severely wounded, and Otoo escaped, with a few of his friends, to the summits of the mountains, where his father and family had taken refuge upon being informed of the defeat. Waheadooa marched directly to Matavae and Oparre, laying waste all the country, as is usual in their wars; but he sent reasonable proposals of peace to Happae and Otoo, who readily accepted them."

Tutaha's war and death occurred in March, 1773, and was the first news received by Captain Cook when he returned to Tahiti on his second voyage and anchored, August 17, in Pihaa Bay, in Vehiatua's territory. Vehiatua himself had died in the interval, and his son, then seventeen or eighteen years of age, had succeeded to the name and authority.

The death of Tutaha and Tepau i Ahurai produced a new revolution, or, perhaps, dissolved the old alliances. Vehiatua of Tiarapu, Teriirere of Papara, Terii Vaetua of Ahurai, and Tunuieaaiteatua of Pare existed henceforward as equals; but of them all, Tu was the least powerful. The only sign that his position had improved was his immediate appearance at Matavai to receive Cook and beg for presents. Apparently the death of Tutaha brought the district of Haapape in some way within the influence or control of Tu, for no chief, except an unknown Toppere (Tiipaarii), was mentioned as ruling there either by Cook or Forster; but Amo and Purea again appeared there in company with Tu and the chiefs of Paea and Tefana, Poatatou and Towha. At that time, therefore, all these chiefs were on friendly terms. Forster said that Teriirere was then married to the eldest sister of Tn, whom he called Neehourai, but he seems to have meant the sister of Tu's wife, who would have been a Tetua i Ahurai, and was the elder sister of Terii Vaetua of Ahurai. We know nothing of such a marriage, and at that time Teriirere was not much more than twelve years old, while Neehourai was thirty.

Tu appeared to Cook to enjoy no great consideration and to be secretly intriguing to gain power. He wanted Cook to help him against Vehiatua and he complained that the chiefs of Ahurai and Paea were not his friends. Although he was engaged, or expected to be engaged, with both these chiefs in a war with Eimeo, he did not command the expedition or take any part in it. The English, who could not conceive that any people should be able to exist without some pretense of concentrated authority, gave to Tu the rank and title of King, while remarking that he was merely one, and not the most important, of several Arii rahi.

Of Papara and its chiefs they saw little, and thought less. Lieutenant Pickersgill, at the end of August, 1773, went as far as Papara, "where O Ammo, who had once been the king of all Taheitee, resided with his son, the young T'-Aree Derre. He took up his first night's lodging on the borders of a small district which was now the property of the famous queen, o-Poorea (Oberea). As soon as she heard of his arrival she hastened to him, and met her old acquaintance with repeated marks of friendship. She had separated from her husband some time after the departure of Captain Wallis, and was now entirely deprived of that greatness which had once rendered her conspicuous in story and august in the eyes of Europeans."

To a Tahitian, who knew what was the usual fate of chiefesses after their sons had taken their rank and their husbands had taken new wives, even though he knew nothing of the position of English dowagers, this peculiarly conventional English morality would have seemed wasted. Purea was still, according to Forster, in the possession of her district, but apparently Papara had taken part in Tutaha's war against Taiarapu, and had been ravaged like Matavai and Pare, in revenge, by Vehiatua. "The civil wars between the two peninsulas of the island had stripped her, as well as the whole district of Paparra, of the greatest part of her wealth, so that she complained to the lieutenant that she was poor (teetee) and had not a hog to give her friends." Pickersgill reported to Cook that "she seemed much altered for the worse, poor and of little consequence. The first words she said to Mr Pickersgill were, Earre mataou ina boa, Earee is frightened, you can have no hogs. By this it appeared that she had little or no property, and was herself subject to the Earee, which I believe was not the case when I was here before. "

The English never took an idea by halves. Having made a queen of Purea in 1768, they were determined to regard her as a beggar in 1773. Nevertheless, Teriirere was still Arii rahi; Papara and the Teva districts were no more changed than their neighbors; in May, 1774, Purea appeared on board Cook's ship at Matavai with the usual presents, and both she and Amo took the same social position they had always held; but the glamour of royalty was gone. "On the 12th [May, 1774]," wrote Cook "old Oberea, the woman, who, when the Dolphin was here in 1767, was thought to be queen of the island, and whom I had not seen since 1769, paid us a visit, and brought a present of hogs and fruit." Forster gave a longer account of this visit. "O-Poorea (Oberea), once the queen of Taheitee, came on board and presented two hogs to Captain Cook. The fame of our red feathers had reached to the plains of Paparra, for she told us she was come to have some of them. She appeared to be between forty and fifty; her per-son was tall, large and fat, and her features, which seemed once to have been more agreeable, were now rather masculine. However, something of her former greatness remained; she had 'an eye to threaten or command,' and a free and noble deportment. She did not stay long on board, probably because she felt herself of less consequence in our eyes than formerly. After enquiring for her friends of the Endeavor, she went ashore in her canoe. O-Ammo likewise came to the ship about this time, but was still less noticed than his late consort; and, being little known on board, was not permitted to come even into the Captain's cabin. It was with difficulty that he could dispose of his hogs, as we had now so many on deck that we did not care to crowd the decks with more. These two royal personages are living examples of the instability of human grandeur."

There could be but one King, and he was Tu of Pare. The chance that made Matavai the most convenient harbor for the English ships made Tu the most important person on the island to provide fresh meat for the English crews. Tu, therefore, greatly to the disgust of the other chiefs, got most of the axes and other gifts, and all the social civilities of the British. This jealousy almost roused a serious fight at Pare, where Tu's rivals for Cook's favor became so violent that Tu himself fled from his own district to Matavai for safety. The Ahurai and Attahuru people were furious, and Cook was quite unable to understand that they had reason to be so. Ahurai and Paea had never before been treated as the inferiors of a Purionuu chief, and they could understand Cook's conduct as little as Cook could understand theirs. To them Cook's infatuation for Tu must have seemed a deliberate insult.

Cook's conduct must have been the more irritating because the chiefs of Ahurai and Paea were then preparing all their forces for an attack on Mahine of

Eimeo and wanted Tu's assistance, which was necessary for their success. They had the whole force of Paea, numbering one hundred and sixty war-canoes; they had forty-four war-canoes from Ahurai, and even had ten from Matavai but they had none from Pare Arue; yet Tu was as closely interested in the result of the war as they could be. As usual, the Eimeo war was a family quarrel, as the opposite table shows. Mahine of Opunohu was an uncle of Teriitapunui of Vavari. Both of them belonged to the Ahurai family, but for some reason not now to be understood Mahine had quarreled with his nephew. Tetuanui, Tu's wife, was sister of Teriitapunui, and would naturally support her brother against their uncle; but although her family, under the lead of Towha, or Tahua, together with the chief of Paea, collected their strength to support Terii ta punui, Tu could not be induced to aid them. When Cook left the island, in May, 1774, the Eimeo war was about to begin. When he returned on his third voyage, in 1777, it was still going on, and Tu was still evading the demand for his assistance. Towha was, in consequence, obliged to make peace with Mahine, and was reported to intend turning his arms against Tu, to punish him. Cook then deliberately intervened in support of the policy he had adopted of elevating Tu at the expense of the other chiefs. In his eyes Tu was King by divine right, and any attack on his authority was treason in the first place and an attack on British influence in the next.

"The terms [of the peace]," said Cook, in his report, "were disadvantageous to Otaheite, and much blame was thrown upon Otoo, whose delay in sending reinforcements had obliged Towha to submit to a disgraceful accommodation. It was even currently reported that Towha, resenting his not being supported, had declared that as soon as I should leave the island he would join his forces to those of Tiaraboo and attack Otoo at Matavai or Oparre. This called upon me to declare in the most public manner that I was determined to espouse the interest of my friend against any such combination, and that whoever presumed to attack him should feel the weight of my heavy displeasure when I returned again to their island. My declaration probably had the desired effect. "

Papara seems to have had nothing to do with these quarrels. The first news Cook had received on his return, in August, 1777, was of Purea's death, which seems to have occurred in 1775 or 1776. Amo had then another wife, taken, like Purea, from the Ahurai family. Her name was Taurua i Ahurai, a cousin of Purea, and she had a son, Temarii, best known in our family by the name of Arii fataia. According to Cook, Purea's son Teriirere was still alive, and in that case must have been chief of Papara. Cook's officers saw him at Faaa, when Towha and Tu met to reconcile their quarrel, in September 1777. He was received by the chief's daughter, his cousin, with the ceremony of cutting her head with the shark's tooth and shedding tears. When Cook was at Opunohu in Eimeo. October 1, he had an account of Amo's death, but on that point the accounts are very contradictory. All I can say is that, as far as I know, Teriirere died unmarried; certainly without heirs; and that he was succeeded as chief of Papara by his half-brother, the Temarii Arii fataia.

Nearly eleven years passed before another European ship visited Tahiti, and during this interval Pomare paid dearly for the prominence his English friends had given him. When Captain Bligh arrived in the Bounty, in 1788, Tu told him "that after five years from the time of Captain Cook's departure (counting sixty-three moons)," that is, at the end of 1782, "the people of the island Eimeo joined with those of Attahooroo, and made a descent on Oparre." Many of Tu's people had been killed; he had himself fled, with the rest, to the mountains; all the houses and property had been destroyed or carried away, and even in 1788 the people "had no other habitations than light sheds which might be taken by the four corners and removed by four men; and of the many large canoes which they then had [in 1777], not more than three remained." Ahurai and Paea seem therefore to have respected Cook's threat for five years; and when they came to the conclusion that he would not return, they took the promised revenge.

CHAPTER XI

I come now to the year 1788, when Lieutenant William Bligh was sent by the British Government in H. M. ship Bounty to bring breadfruit from Tahiti, to be domesticated as a fruit of peculiar usefulness in the various tropical colonies of Great Britain. The Voyage of the Bounty has become as classical as the Voyages of Cook and Bougainville. More books and essays have been written about the Bounty than about any other two-hundred-ton ship whose crew ever mutinied, before or since; but the part of its story which was most serious to us is the part which has been least noticed by the world. What Bligh said to Christian, and what Christian said to Bligh, and what Peter Heywood said to both, and how Thursday October Christian made his dramatic appearance at Pitcairn Island, and a thousand other details of the picturesque story, have been told a hundred times, and always to interested audiences; but no one has taken the trouble to tell how great an influence Bligh and his mutineers exercised over the destinies of Tahiti, and especially of its old chiefs.

Bligh had been the master of Cook's ship, the Resolution, on Cook's third and last voyage. He came back in 1788 with all the ideas which Cook had fixed on his mind in 1777. Had he been a Frenchman, he might perhaps have enjoyed discovering the mistakes of his predecessors, and trying to correct them by mistakes of his own, but when the English once saw what they took to be a fact, they saw nothing else forever. Bligh appeared at Matavai in the Bounty, October 26, 1788, without a doubt that his old acquaintance, Otoo, was King of all Tahiti, and a friend of King George III, to be upheld against every attack, aristocratic or democratic; and what with Cook had been chiefly a matter of convenience and policy became with Bligh a simple matter of course.

Yet the situation in which Bligh found Tu would have roused doubts in the mind of any one except a sailor or a soldier. Tu was almost at his last gasp when the Bounty arrived. Pare Arue had been thoroughly ravaged and plundered; everything that Cook gave to Tu had been carried away; a cow was at Faaa; the bull was at Hitiaa; a chest which had been made expressly for Tu, large enough for him and his wife to sleep on, was said to be in Eimeo. Apparently the whole body of Tu's neighbors had united to punish and impoverish him. Bligh remarked that although Tu went with him to Faaa, he did not land, but remained in the boat, and received no sign of respect, nor even a cocoanut or a breadfruit. He would not go with Bligh to Eimeo on any terms, "but said that, notwithstanding my protection, he was certain the Eimeo people would watch for an opportunity to kill him." He stood in fear even of his half-brother Ariipaea, who seemed to. be much the more respected of the two; and the chief of Matavai, Poeeno, told Bligh that Tu and his brother Ariipaea "were not on good terms together, and it was imagined that they would fight as soon as the ship was gone." Tu's position was so desperate that he begged Bligh to take him and his wife, Tetua, to England, and Bligh was at some loss for an excuse.

"To quiet his importunity, I was obliged to promise that I would ask the king's permission to carry them to England if I came again; that then I should be in a larger ship and could have accommodations properly fitted up. I was sorry to find that Tinah [Tu] was apprehensive he should be attacked by his enemies as soon as our ship left Otaheite, and that if they joined they would be too powerful for him. The illness of Teppahoo [Tepau of Ahurai], with whom he was on good terms, gave him much uneasiness -- Teppaho's wife being a sister of Otow's and aunt to Tinah. They have no children, ... and if Teppahoo were to die, he would be succeeded as Earee of the district of Tettaha [Ahurai] by his brother, who is an enemy of Tinah. I have on every occasion endeavored to make the principal people believe that we should return again to Otaheite, and that we should revenge any injury done in our absence to the people of Matavai and Oparre."

Another event had helped to diminish the dignity of Tu in the eyes of foreigners:

"I was surprised to find that instead of Otoo, the name by which he formerly went, he was now called Tinah. The name of Otoo, with the title of Earee rahie [Arii rahi], I was informed, had devolved to his eldest son, who was yet a minor, as is the custom of the country. I prepared a magnificent present for this youth, who was represented to me as the person of the greatest consequence or, rather, of the highest rank in the island."

Bligh was allowed to see the young Tu only across a river. The child appeared to be about six years old. He was therefore born about 1782, and this is our first glimpse of our first Christian king.

Old Tu, or Tinah, was very anxious that Bligh should redeem Cook's pledge and punish the Eimeo people, but succeeded only in persuading him at least not to encourage them by a friendly visit. Bligh seemed neither to see nor to act, except in the directions that Tu wished. He would not actually engage in war, but he showed not the slightest interest or curiosity in any one but the Tus, father and son, and their immediate connexion. Tu's half-brother, Ariipaia, son of old Teu by a second wife (see Table VII), attracted Bligh's attention chiefly because he was said to be Tu's enemy. Teppaho, or Tepau, the chief of Ahurai, received notice because he was Tu's friend. Further than this Bligh neither looked nor asked. He seems neither to have known nor cared who were the chiefs of Eimeo, Paea, or Hitiaa, who had destroyed Tu's power and seized his property. He scarcely mentioned the remoter and more powerful chiefs of Papara and Taiarapu. From his book we get no light except on the subject of Tu, and even for that we must be grateful.

Before leaving the island, April 3, 1789, Bligh did what he could to protect the man whose position was alternately made and destroyed by British patronage. If Tu's situation had not been tragical to the island, it would have been comical. As long as British ships were in Matavai Bay, he was rich and powerful; his house was filled with all that made wealth: axes, fish-hooks, cloth, nails, beads; and cattle, goats, or whatever the ships contained. No other chief received gifts except in trifling amounts. The instant the British ships disappeared, this wealth became an irresistible temptation to Tu's neighbors and a fatal danger to himself. Tu had been a sort of milch-cow to the chiefs of Eimeo, Faaa, and Hitiaa. He begged the gifts which they were to squeeze from him. Knowing Tu's situation and dangers, Bligh gave him arms:

"He had frequently expressed a wish that I would leave some firearms and ammunition with him, as he expected to be attacked after the ship sailed, and perhaps chiefly on account of our partiality to him: I therefore thought it but reasonable to accede to his request; and I was the more readily prevailed on, as he said his intentions were to act only on the defensive. This indeed seems most suited to his disposition, which is neither active nor enterprising. If Tinah had spirit in proportion to his size and strength, he would probably be the greatest warrior in Otaheite; but courage is not the most conspicuous of his virtues. When I proposed to leave with him a pair of pistols, which they prefer to muskets, the told me that Iddeah [Tefua, his wife] would fight with one and Oedidee [Itiiti] with the other. Iddeah has learnt to load and fire a musket with great dexterity, and Oedidee is an excellent marksman. It is not common for women in this country to go to war, but Iddeah is a very resolute woman, of a large make, and has great bodily strength."

Having done what he could to protect Tu, Bligh sailed from the island April 4, and was passing the Friendly, or Tonga, group April 28, when the larger part of his officers and crew mutinied and set him and some eighteen others adrift in the ship's launch. The mutineers then put theship about and returned to Tahiti, where they arrived at Ma-tavai Bay June 6, 1789. There they took in all the live-stock they could get, and twenty-four Tahitians, and sailed again, June 16, for Tubuai, but appeared once more, September 22, and landed sixteen of the mutineers who were weary of their adventures. The rest sailed suddenly the next night, and vanished for twenty years from the sight of men.

The sixteen mutineers who had landed at Matavai scattered more or less over the island, but mostly stayed at Pare with Tu, their patron; and there they set to work November 12, 1789, to build a thirty-foot schooner, in order to escape. The schooner was launched August 5, 1790.

These dates are rather interesting because they fix a few points which would without them be very uncertain. The war which immediately followed, and which reestablished Tu for the moment in his fortunes, deserves to be called the War of the Mutineers of the Bounty. When Tu died, thirteen years later, the missionaries entered in their Journal many details about his life and character; and among other things they said:

"He was born in the district of Oparre, where his corpse now is, and was by birth chief of that, district, and none other. The notice of the English navigators laid the foundation for his future aggrandisement; and the runaway seamen that from time to time quitted their vessels to sojourn in the island (especially that part of his Majesty's ship Bounty's crew which resided here), were the instruments for gaining to Pomarre a greater extent of dominion and power than any man ever had before in Otaheite."

Tu began by asking the mutineers to go with him to Eimeo and fight Mahine. They refused, but cleaned his guns, which enabled him, by aid of Itiiti, to win a success. Mahine then came over to Faaa and united with Towha of Faaa, and Potatow of Paea to resist Tu's next attack.

This War of the Mutineers of the Bounty, which occurred soon after the schooner was launched, August, 5, 1790, brings Papara again into notice, for this time the chief of Papara joined Tu against Faaa, Paea and Eimeo. The mutineers brought their schooner and their guns, with Tu's canoes, from Pare round to Paea, and fought a battle which was decided by the death of Mahine, killed by Tu's brother-in-law, Terii Vaetua. The chiefs of Paea and Ahurai, defeated in battle, unable to face the guns of the mutineers and of Tu's men; hemmed in on the north by Tu and the mutineers; on the south by Temarii and more Englishmen from Papara, fled at last to the hills and submitted to the conqueror.

This was about September, 1790. Tu's English arms and English seamen had at last enabled him to effect a part of his ambitious purpose, and to crush Eimeo, Ahurai and Paea; but one of our family reads with astonishment that Papara helped him. Who was, then, the Temarii who ruled at Papara in 1790? To answer this question I shall need a whole chapter by itself. The English, who were conscious, whenever their interest required it, that a chief of Papara still existed, never cared to ask who he was. They had never heard of any chiefs of Papara except Amo, Purea and Teriirere, and in their accounts, whenever a chief of Papara was mentioned, he was invariably translated as Amo, or as Teriirere, the son of Amo and Purea. Yet, beyond doubt, when the war of 1790 occurred, Amo, Purea and Teriirere were all dead. Even the brief notices of Papara, which were called out by the visit of the frigate Pandora, show that a new chief must have ruled at Papara.

The Pandora frigate belongs also to the tale of the mutineers rather than to the history of the island. When Lieutenant Bligh reached home and reported the mutiny, the British government sent the frigate Pandora in search of the Bounty. The Pandora never found the Bounty, which had long since been burned by the mutineers at Pitcairn island; but she did find such of the mutineers as had returned to Tahiti, who were actively engaged in establishing Tu as a Tahitian despot when the Pandora, in March, 1791, appeared in Matavai Bay. Those of the mutineers who were at Pare, under Tu's direct power, were easily recovered, but Captain Edwards, of the Pandora, found that some of the others had "claimed protection of Tamatrah, a great chief in Papara, who was the proper king of Otaheite, the present family of Otoo being usurpers, and who intended, had we not arrived, with the assistance of the Bounty's people, to have disputed the point with Otoo". "Captain Edwards had taken every possible means of gaining the friendship of Tamarah, the great prince of the upper district, by sending him very liberal presents, which effectually brought him over to our interest."

Captain Edwards made an official report of his own, dated from Batavia, Nov. 25, 1791, in which he said much about Tu and Temarii. The mutineers, it seems, unable to keep at sea in their schooner, landed at Papara, March 26, and took refuge in the mountains. Captain Edwards immediately sent two boats, with a number of men, to Papara. His report continued:

"I found the Otoo ready to furnish me with guides and to give me any other assistance in his power, but he has very little authority or influence in that part of the island where the pirates had taken refuge and even his right to the sovereignty of the eastern part of the island had been recently disputed by Tamarie, one of the royal family. Under these circumstances I conceived the taking Otoo and the other chiefs attached to his interest into custody would alarm the faithful part of his subjects and operate to our disadvantage. I therefore satisfied myself with the assistance he offered and had in his power to give me and I found means at different times to convey presents to Tamarie (and invited him to come on board which he promised to do but never fulfilled his promise), and convinced him I had it in my power to lay his country waste, which I imagined would be sufficient at least to make him withhold that support he hitherto through policy had occasionally given to the pirates in order to draw them to his interest and strengthen his own party against the Otoo. I probably might have had it in my power to have taken and secured the person of Tamarie, but I was apprehensive that such an attempt might irritate the natives attached to his interest and induce them to act hostilely against our party at a time the ship was at too great a distance to afford them timely and necessary assistance."

The reasons of all naval officers, as far as the history of Tahiti is concerned, have been very much alike, no matter what their nationality or their object; so I need not dwell on those which led Captain Edwards to spare the lives and property of Tahitians, whether Tevas or Purionuu, who had given him no kind of offence. The end of it was that the mutineers were brought in, one by one, until only six remained out. Captain Edwards sent two parties to find them. One party went by sea to Papara, under Lieut. Hayward. "The old Otoo and several of the Chiefs, etc., went with him." The other party crossed through the mountains. "Oripaia, the Otoo's brother, went with him." The mutineers were found near the sea-shore, and surrendered.

From these extracts, it appears that the Chief of Papara, in March and April, 1791, was as powerful, as independent, and as hostile to the ambition of Tu, as any previous Temarii had been, and that neither Tu nor Tu's half brother Ariipaea then ventured to exercise, or even to have exercised within a year past any authority or influence at Papara.

Down to April, 1791, we may conclude that no change had taken place in the relative position of the Chief of Papara towards the Chief of Pare Arue. Such changes as had taken place regarded Eimeo and Taiarapu, but these were very serious, and must have been very alarming to the Inner Tevas. What we know of them comes chiefly from the Voyage of Vancouver who arrived at the island at the close of the same year.

The Pandora sailed, with her prisoners, from Tahiti in May, 1791; and in the following December Vancouver arrived, in the sloop-of-war Discovery, on a search for the Northwest Passage. Stopping for refreshment at Tahiti, December 28, Vancouver, who had been with Cook in 1777, enquired for his old friends:

"I had the mortification of finding, on inquiry, that most of the friends I had left here in the year 1777, both male and female, were dead, Otoo, with his father [Teu], brothers, and sisters; Potatow and his family, were the only chiefs of my old acquaintance that were now living. Otoo was not here [at Pare]; nor did it appear that Otaheite was now the place of his residence, having retired to his newly acquired possession, Eimeo, or, as the natives more commonly call that island, Morea, leaving his eldest son the supreme authority over this and all the neighboring islands. The young king had taken the name of Otoo and my old friend that of Pomurrey, having given up his name with his sovereign jurisdiction, though he still seemed to retain his authority as regent."

This is the first record of the name Pomare, by which the family has been since known. After the birth of the young Tu, about 1782, the first of his children who was allowed to live, the father seems to have taken the name of Tinah, perhaps Taino, which he bore in 1788. He took the name of Po-mare (night-cough) from his younger son, Terii navahoroa, a very young child in 1791, who coughed at night. Subsequently he took the name of Vatratoa, as I shall notice in its place, and as Vairatoa he is still known in the family.

Vancouver sent a boat to Eimeo for Pomare, who came over January 2, 1792, bringing with him his brother-in-law Motuaria, or Metuaro, who was supposed by Vancouver to be the same Terii tapunui that was known to Cook and Forster as chief of Varari in Eimeo. He was called commonly Metuaro Mahau. According to our records, he was Taaro-arii, a younger brother of Cook's Terii tapunui, who was dead without issue, and left his name and property to Taaro-arii, who also had no male children.

"With Pomurrey," said Vancouver, came Matuara Mahau, "the reigning prince, under Otoo, of Morea. There was, however, little probability of his long enjoying this honorable station, as he appeared to be in the last stage of a deep and rapid decline."

In fact Motuaria died ten days afterwards, and, according to Vancouver, left his chieferies in Eimeo to a daughter, Pomare's niece; "to this young princess Pomurrey became regent, and in course the inhabitants of Morea were entirely at his command." Thus Tu had accomplished his first great object, the extending of his power over Eimeo, or at least one-half of it.

The next step, the acquisition of Taiarapu, had followed the victory at Attahuru, and Vancouver was able to record it. His account, probably given him by Pomare's own people, began with the war of 1790, in which Mahine perished and the chiefs of Faaa and Paea were conquered.

"Maheine having fallen in this conflict [at Attahuru] and Towha [of Ahurai] being dead, little was necessary to complete the conquest [of Mahine's district, Opunohu in Eimeo], which was finally accomplished by the excursion of the Bounty's people in a vessel they had constructed from the timber of the breadfruit tree; and as good or bad fortune is generally attended with corroborating events, other circumstances intervened to foster and indulge the ambition of Pomurrey. At this time Whyeadooa [Vehiatua], the king of Taiarabou, died leaving only a very distant relation to assume his name and government; who was by Pomurrey and his adherents obliged to relinquish all pretensions to such honors, and with the people of Taiarabou to acknowledge Pomurrey's youngest son as their chief, under the authority of his eldest son, Otoo, which, on their assenting to, the youth assumed the name of Whyeadooa as a necessary appendage to the government. By this acquisition, it should appear, they have more effectually established a firm and lasting peace among themselves than has been enjoyed for a long series of years; and to insure this inestimable blessing to their dominions, the royal brothers have so disposed themselves as completely to watch over and protect the two young princes during their minority. Urripiah [Ariipaea], the next brother [half-brother] to Pomurrey, having acquired the reputation of a great warrior, has taken up his residence on the borders of Taiarabou to watch the conduct of those people in their allegiance to his nephew Whyeadooa, and on the least appearance of disaffection or revolt, to be at hand for pursuing such measures as may be required to bring them back to their obedience. Whytooa [Vaetua], the next brother [brother-in-law], resides for the like reason at Oparre, near the young monarch; and Pomurrey with his wives has retired to Morea, where the inhabitants are in all respects perfectly reconciled, firmly attached to his interest, and ready to afford him and his children every support and assistance they may require."

From this account it is clear that, by means of the English and their firearms, Pomare had succeeded in destroying the rival chiefs of Opunohu, Faaa, and Taiarapu, but he still kept an ominous silence about the most serious rival of all, the chief of Papara, whose fate was to come last. What sort of peace Pomare wanted was clear to Vancouver, for, as the irresistible power of the English guns became more and more evident, Pomare's views became more extensive, until they embraced all the islands within reach, including Borabora.

"Pomurrey and his brothers, having procured from the vessels which had lately visited Otaheite several muskets and pistols, they considered themselves invincible; and the acquiring new possessions for Otoo now seemed to occupy the whole of their study and attention. They were extremely solicitous that I should contribute to their success by augmenting their number of fire-arms, and adding to their stock of ammunition. Of the latter I gave Pomurrey a small quantity; but of the former I had none to dispose of, even if I had seen no impropriety in complying with his request. Finding there was no prospect of increasing their armory, they requested that I would have the goodness to conquer the territories on which they meditated a descent, and, having so done, to deliver them up to Otoo; and as an excuse for their subjugation insisted that it was highly essential to the comfort and happiness of the people at large that over the whole group of these islands there should be only one sovereign. On satisfying them that the islands in question were quite out of my route, and that I had no leisure for such an enterprise, Pomurrey in the most earnest manner requested that on my return to England I would in his name solicit His Majesty to order a ship, with proper force, to be immediately sent out, with directions that if all those islands were not subjected to his power before her arrival she was to conquer them for Otoo, who, he observed, I well knew would ever be a steady friend to King George and the English. This request was frequently repeated, and he did not fail to urge it in the most pressing manner at our parting."

In all this account nothing shows that the people of Tahiti were more reconciled than they had previously been to the supremacy of Tu. That he was still afraid of the Tevas of Taiarapu and Papara was plain; but he had secured one advantage that gave him a distinction he had never enjoyed before. Besides the Ura or red feathers, which were the exclusive signs of the Arii rahi, a curious form of the Maro ura had been made the symbol of supreme authority by Purea. This was the British pennant left flying at Matavai by Captain Wallis at his departure. Purea took it to her Marae of Mahaiatea, and seems to have converted it into the Maro ura with which her son was to be invested. On her overthrow Tutaha took it to his own Marae of Maraetaata as the symbol of his supremacy. There Cook saw it, ornamented with red, yellow, and black feathers. There it remained from 1768 to 1790, when Pomare, having conquered Paea, at last gained possession of the Maro ura, and carried it away to his own Marae i Tarahoi in Pare. Whether he could keep it, depended on the English guns.

CHAPTER XII

I must now come to the question I have already asked myself: Who was the chief of Papara who joined Tu against Paea and helped Tu to seize the chieferies of Ahurai and Taiarapu and the sovereignty over Opunohu, as well as the Maro ura which belonged to Papara and had never till then been beyond the control of Tevahitua?

Certainly the chief was not Teriirere, the son of Purea. Teriirere was dead, and neither wife nor child of his is known to tradition. Purea seems to have had no other child by Amo. Teriirere had been born about 1762, and as early as 1769 Cook knew that Amo and Purea had long been separated by mutual consent. Like other chiefs, Amo took other wives, and apparently the treaty of 1768-9, by which Tutaha restored peace and punished Purea, stipulated that Amo should marry another Ahurai chiefess. Cook supposed this contract was for Teriirere, but the English were invariably confused in their attempts to understand native ranks and relationships. In 1774 Forster saw much of Vaetua, who told him that his eldest sister, whose name Forster wrote Tedua Neehourai -- Tetua i Ahurai -- who seemed to be about thirty years old, was married to the son oi Amo, called Teriirere, who was then a child of twelve. In truth, she probably was married to Amo himself, for we know by our family records that he married Taurua i Ahurai, a niece of Purea and a cousin of Tu's wife. By her he had another son, Temarii, known to us as Ariifaataia, who was born apparently about 1772, and was therefore some ten years younger than Teriirere and ten years older than Tu's son, our later King Pomare. Whenever Teriirere died, he was succeeded by Ariifaataia.

At this point comes in a curious story heard forty years afterwards by Moerenhout, and printed in his book. Moerenhout was the only writer about Tahiti who knew Papara well; was on intimate terms with Tati, the next chief, my grandfather, and got from him much of what he afterwards put in his book. Unfortunately Moerenhout seldom mentioned his authorities, and had more than a reasonable weakness for confusing names, dates and events. While his story seems to be as precise as any one could wish, it is really difficult to follow.

"At the death of Amo," says Moerenhout, "which happened shortly before the appearance of the Bounty [October 26, 1788, June 6 or September 22, 1789], his son, then named Oripaea, being still too young to command, Ariifaataia, Amo's brother, was named as regent."

I venture to correct this, so as to read as follows: At the death of the chief of Papara, which happened before 1788, Amo's next son, Ariifaataia, being only fifteen or sixteen years old, Ariipaea, who had married Amo's niece, was named as guardian. A glance at Table VII will show how this guardianship affected the situation of Papara.

Ariipaea, as Bligh knew him in 1788, was Tu's half-brother, an active, useful man about thirty-six years old, supposed not to be on good terms with Tu. Three years afterwards, in 1791, Vancouver found him in the most important and confidential relation with Tu, having taken up his residence on the borders of Taiarapu, to guard against revolt or disaffection in the south. He died some five years afterwards, and the heir to his name and estates seems to have been Ariifaataia.

Returning now to Moerenhout's version of the story, and reading Ariipaea for Ariifaataia, with the assumption that Ariipaea had become guardian in 1787, and knowing that the mutineers of the Bounty did not establish themselves in Tahiti until September 22, 1789, the course of events seems to become intelligible.

"He [Ariipaea] was a weak man who allowed himself to be influenced by Otou, and contributed to his elevation by remaining inactive while the latter attacked Taiarabou and the other districts. When, therefore, sustained by the mutineers of the English war-vessel, Otou, Pornare or Tinah dreamed [in 1790] of conquering the whole island, he sought first to conciliate Ariipaea, who disposed of a considerable force, and who had joined with Vehiatua, or Te arii navaoroa, of Taiarabou against whom Pomare wished to act first. To neutralize this alliance, which alarmed him, Pomare sent to Ariipaea considerable presents, among which he did not forget to slip some objects of European manufacture; and sent word to him, through his vea, or messenger, that he looked on him as a father; wanted to be his ally -- his friend -- and wished to make him a visit, both to seek his advice and to form an alliance that should be as durable as it was close."

In fact Ariipaea was ten years younger than Tu, and his weakness may well be doubted, if, as is alleged, he betrayed his trust, and sold his ward's interests to Tu, his brother. Of the fact, I do not doubt, and, in spite of apparent difficulties in dates, Moerenhout's story is, in my belief, more or less an exact version of old Tati's words.

"Flattered by this condescension from so formidable a rival, the old man [Ariipaea] forgot himself; and, sacrificing the interests of his pupil [Ariifaataia], sent word at once to Pomare that he was expecting him; that he would cede to him his own place in the Marae; that he would prepare his food, &c.; all expressions which among these people imply, more than tacitly, submission and servitude."

Accordingly, a few days afterwards Pomare set out, with a numerous suite and with all the pomp that chiefs employed on such occasions. The step was taken suddenly, and Ariipaea kept it secret from the people. The first they knew of it was the sight of their enemy, Pomare, approaching with a fleet.

"The day of Pomare's arrival had not been fixed, and he was wholly unexpected, when, one morning, a numerous fleet was seen advancing. Fearing at first some surprise, the people ran to arms, but they soon saw that those in the canoes were unarmed, and that in one of the leading boats was the chief Pomare. Yet, when informed of the intended transaction, which they disapproved, and knowing also what ceremonies would be practiced on this visit, the people retired to the mountains, taking the women and children, and in a few minutes there remained on the shore only two sick people who could not move. This retreat threw the chiefs into extreme embarrassment, for victims were absolutely necessary -- three at least. For want of better, they sacrificed the two sick persons and carried them near the Marae. The survivors were all chiefs or priests, and knew not where to find the third victim, when all eyes turned on an old and intimate friend of the chief. This very quality and his age pointed him out to the executioners; so, without a word, the only question was who should strike him the first blow, and, in spite of his cries and prayers, he was put with the two other victims. When Pomare touched the shore, they brought the three bodies and rolled them under his canoe, he being in it, taking the greatest care not to let him touch the land. Then from there the canoe was carried by the chiefs of Papara and by his own people into the Marae, where Ariipaea and the servants of the temple were waiting. When the train reached the interior, Ariipaea, seated on the altar, invited Pomare to take his place, and put himself at Pomare's feet. The grand-priest then began the ceremony, offered the victims to the gods, tore out an eye from one, which he offered to Pomare, withdrawing it, as was the custom, and, after long prayers, addressed himself to the new sovereign, offering him in the name of Ariipaea the lands of the district of Papara. The descendants of Amo and Berea had till then been nearly always the chiefs of the isle, and since several generations their ancestors occupied the throne, or took rank among the most powerful chiefs. Pomare, whose family, on the contrary, had never been one of the most considered or most influential, became by the submission of Ariipaea master of the peninsula called O-tainee, and prepared to march at once on Taiarabou, the other peninsula of Otaiti, whose chief, Vaiatua or Te arii navaora, far from submission, had himself pretensions to supremacy. In consequence of this opposition, Pomare thought he had best make sure of the conquest of Taiarabou, but he still kept his views in regard to Eimeo. The English, who had brought from the Bounty many more guns and munitions than they needed, gave some of them to the chief and his subjects, some of whom had learned the use of fire-arms. Profiting by this advantage, they attacked the island, got rid of the chief, and hastened to restore Motou Aro, Pomare's old ally, who had been long exiled from the place where his family had ruled from time immemorial."

The impression made on the people of Papara by Ariipaea's betrayal of his trust was profound. They had no share in it, and seem never to have recognized it as binding upon them. Pomare's reception at the Marae of Mataoa must have been before August, 1790, when the mutineers launched their schooner, yet when Edwards arrived in the Pandora in March, 1791, he instantly discovered not only that Tu was without authority or influence at Papara, but that Temarii of Papara had recently been threatening to drive Tu out of his own district of Pare. To reconcile these facts, we must suppose that Ariifaataia had come of age early in 1790, immediately after Ariipaea's homage. The next that was said about Temarii was told by the missionaries of the Duff, who reached Tahiti in March, 1797. They got the story from two Swedes; Andrew Lind of the ship Matilda, which had been wrecked in these seas in 1792; and Peter Haggerstein, who deserted from the Daedalus in February, 1793. Both these men were beach-combers of the type that has infested the South Seas for a century; they became prominent in our history, sometimes helping the missionaries and sometimes annoying them; scoundrels of the sea-going sort; boasters and liars as well as murderers; but from their talk we can sift out some grains of truth, and some idea of the miserable condition of the island.

In July, 1797, Peter the Swede accompanied one of the missionaries on a circuit round the island to make a sort of census, as a starting-point for the missionary work. They began with Papenoo, July 11, and as they walked Peter boasted of his exploits. The first war, he said, happened in 1793, when he had been but five months on the island. Peter had deserted from the Daedalus in February 1793; the war, therefore, took place in July, 1793; but the war which he went on to describe was that of 1790, which he could only have known from hearsay, and which he told with a strange jumble of fact and fiction. According to him, Pomare had begun by attacking Papenoo, and hiring Peter and Andrew and "the Jew" to shoot for him. With their aid he conquered the east side of the island. Then, Peter continued:

"Still they [Pomare and his son Otoo] had powerful enemies who were meditating a grand attack upon them; these were Wyheatua [Vehiatua], king of Tiaraboo, and Temarre, chief over all the districts on the south side, from the isthmus down to Attahooroo; over the latter district was young Towha, who wished to remain neuter, but was forced by Pomarre to join his party, though he was more inclined to favor Temarre, and was afterwards charged with having secretly concerted matters so as to gain him the battle. Temarre encouraged his men by telling them that he had muskets, powder, ball, and white men, as well as his adversary; and that themselves were more numerous than Otoo's party. The whites he had were Connor, an Irishman, and James Butcher, a Scotchman, both of the Matilda's crew. Accordingly, about a month after the battle of Whapiauno [Papenoo], these powerful adversaries met in the district of Attahooroo, but being afraid of each other in no small degree, the first day was spent and nothing done. In all their movements they surrounded the white men, trusting more in them than ever an Asiatic did in his elephant. On the second day the onset began; but in a short time Towha's men, who were in front, ran away, and all Pomarre's followed their example; which was afterwards charged on Towha as his preconcerted scheme. Peter, Andrew and the Jew, however, stood their ground and shot four men. Butcher and Connor were obliged to run for their lives, and Oammo, the father of Temarre, was killed by a musket shot. These advantages brought their party back to assist them; all their adversaries fled, and a complete victory was gained for Pomarre, whom they found at a great distance from the fight, quite overcome with fear, and lying flat on the ground, held fast by the roots of a tree. When they acquainted him with their success he would hardly believe it, but continued to lie like one out of his senses; so little courage did this chief of the victorious army possess. The routed party fled to the remoter districts; some took refuge in the hills; one man in particular got up a very dangerous precipice and threw large stones on his enemies below, and kept his station till he knew their rage had subsided. The consequence of this battle was that Temarre became subject to the victors; was obliged to give to Otoo the great Morae at Papara; also every other privilege of the supreme chief. A house was built by Otoo in all his districts, where some of his servants constantly reside, and he occasionally visits; they represent his sovereignty, and none dare to pass them without stripping, the same as to himself. However, notwithstanding these things, the power of Temarre was still very great; he was left in possession of all his districts, and exercises the office of chief priest of the Eatooa on that side of the island".

Peter's story closed by summing up the situation in a paragraph that has naturally perplexed the historians who have taken his account seriously.

"Towha being charged with treachery was stripped of his district, and obliged to live as a private man at Pappara. Wyheatua had fled to Tiaraboo, where in a short time after he was defeated, and reduced in a like manner as Towha to a private station, and Otoo's younger brother made prince of his kingdom."

The only point to this long story is that the Swede was a great boaster, which the missionaries knew, and a great liar, which they probably suspected. He was talking about his share in wars fought long before his arrival. Vancouver's narrative has shown that as early as 1790, three years before Peter fought his first battle, Vehiatua was dead, and Pomare had seized Tiarapu. Towha was also dead when Vancouver arrived in December, 1791. The only part of the tale which has a semblance of truth is that Towha was conquered at Paea, and that Otoo was received at Mataoa. These events had occurred in 1790, years before Peter and Andrew reached the islands, for their date was fixed by Vancouver. The fact that in 1791, as in 1797, Temarii was in possession of all his districts, and not at all under the guardianship of Ariipaea, is the only point that we can regard as certain; and this also flatly contradicts Peter's tales to the innocent missionaries about his prowess in battles which he never could have seen.

In respect to Temarii, Peter could not have deceived the missionaries if he would, for they already knew the chief of Papara, as well as Haamanemane of Raiatea, the high-priest of Maraetaata, a personage who figured largely in the drama of the two Pomares. Temarii had come to see the missionaries at Matavai, and they had been told, as usual, that he was the son of Purea, which was near the truth, if, as we are told in our traditions, he was in fact the son of Amo. The missionaries described him with unusually life-like touches.

"May 7th [1797]. Visited by a chief-priest from Papara, Te-marree, who is reputed equal to Manne Manne. He is called an Eatooa, sometimes Taata no t' Eatooa, the man of the Eatooa. He was dressed in a wrapper of Otaheitan cloth, and over it an officer's coat doubled round him. At his first approach he appeared timid, and was invited in. He was but just seated when the cuckoo clock struck and filled him with astonishment and terror. Old Pyetea had brought the bird some bread-fruit, observing it must be starved if we never fed it. At breakfast we invited Temarree to our repast, but he first held out his hand with a bit of plantain and looked very solemn, which one of the natives said was an offering to the Eatooa and we must receive. When we had taken it out of his hand and laid it under the table, he sat down and made a hearty breakfast. Brother Cover read the translated address to all these respected guests, the natives listening with attention, and particularly the priest, who seemed to drink in every word, but appeared displeased when urged to cast away their false gods, and on hearing the names Jehovah and Jesus he would turn and whisper."

Two days afterwards Temarii came again to the mission-house, and this time with the young Otoo, Pomare II, and his first wife, Tetuanui.

"9th. Temarree accompanied the king and queen and staid to dine with us. He is, we find, of the royal race and son of the famed Oberea. He is the first chief of the island after Pomarre, by whom he has been subdued, and now lives in friendship with him and has adopted his son. He is also high in esteem as a priest. "

This was May 9. Temarii must have returned at once to Papara, for two of the missionaries found him there May 14, and reported that they "were most hospitably entertained by Temarree, who prevailed on brother Main to be his tayo, and gave him and brother Clode each a double canoe, showing them all his stores and fire-arms which he got from the mutineers; the guns, however, by the policy of the Swedes, are all bent."

The Swedes must have bent the guns in Pomare's interest, for the treachery would otherwise have been against their own, since they must have been in Temarii's service if he trusted them with the care of the guns, and allowed them a chance to injure his most precious property -- property on which his life depended.

In July two of the missionaries again stopped at Papara, on their way round the island. They had found Pomare at Mataoae, and coming directly from him they arrived the same evening at the house of Te-marii. When they arrived he was sleeping under the influence of kava, and the next morning early went off to his Marae without seeing them. The missionaries walked over to Purea's great Marae at Mahaiatea; then returned and breakfasted on Temarii's guest-pig; and in the afternoon walked on to the westward.

"About a mile along the beach we met Temarre on his way home; and when Peter told him that we had waited purposely for him, he seemed much afraid lest I should be angry, and asked if I was not. On satisfying him that I was not, he then inquired into the cause of our visit to Pomarre in a way that bespoke jealousy, envy and fear of that chief. After a little conversation we parted. Temarre is supposed to be possessed of the Eatooa, and in conformity to that supposition, speaks in such a way that scarcely any one can understand him. This at first made me think that he used that peculiar language said to be spoken by the priests; but both the Swedes insist that the priests know no other than the common language, and can always be understood, except when, for the sake of mysteriousness, they utter their speeches in a singing tone, and that even the young girls can make their songs equally unintelligible, it is also said of this chief that he is now meditating revenge on Pomarre on account of the death of his father and his own defeat; and in hope of obtaining success he has chosen Mr. Main for his tayo, whom he has heard spoken of as a military man, and to whom he has made several great presents."

All this accords well with what Captain Edwards reported in 1791; and with what the missionaries told of Temarii's doings afterwards. Whatever may have been done at Papara by way of submission to Tu, before Ariifaataia came of age, it was not recognised as binding either by Ariifaataia or by the people of the Papara district; but before going on with the story of Ariifaataia I have some few family traditions about this unlucky chief which are best in place here.

CHAPTER XIII

Ariipaea, Tu's half brother, who, as guardian of Papara, sold his rights to Tu, died in 1796 or 1797. His widow, Teriitua, Aromaiterai's daughter, then chiefess of Hitiaa, was commonly known by the English as Inna Madua (Vahine metua), and continued for several years more to make a considerable figure in the family of Pomare. Apparently the Temarii Ariifaataia inherited the name of his guardian and relative, for the missionaries used indifferently the term Temarii or Ariipaea (Orepiah) in speaking of our Papara chief, whom we know in tradition only as Ariifaataia.

Ariifaataia, if the wish of his family had availed, should have married the chiefess of Vaiari, the Maheanuu i Farepua, who was not only socially the first of all Tahiti chiefs, and whose Maraes of Farepua and Tahiti were the oldest on the island, but who was also at that time the acknowledged beauty of Tahiti, whose fame remains a by word to this day. Maheanuu refused to marry Ariifaataia, brilliant as the match was, even for her. She thought him too ugly. Handsome women were then becoming more rare in the island, if Vancouver is to be believed; and Maheanuu was not disposed to throw her beauty away merely for power; yet the marriage was for a time supposed to be arranged, and the Papara people still preserve a song intended to celebrate the occasion:

ARIIFAATAIA AND MAHEANOU

Orie e pati i te pae tahatai

E mahuta mai te aaura i Taravao.

Ei tapihoo itei Terehemanu

Ia vai noa mai te moua iti ra Tearatauru

E Temarii e e oto oe i te moua ra moua Tamaiti.

Orie is a fish, or bait, which attracts the bird Aa-ur-a, the parrot with red feathers, of Taravao, meaning of course the Maheanuu, to change place with the bird Terehe, meaning of course Temarii, and share his mounts of Tearatauru and Tamaiti, his most precious possessions. To translate the song literally would be a hopeless task. Its interest is in its local allusions rather than in its poetry.

The Maheanuu having rejected Ariifaataia for his ugliness, her neighbor, the daughter of the chief of Mataiea, became his wife. This was a family connection. Mauaroa, chief of Mataiea, had married Teraiautia of the Aromaiterai family. Their daughter bore several names: Tetuaraenui o Teva; Pipiri; Fareahu; Teriitahi. The missionaries, in their census of the island, in July, 1797, called Temarii's wife Tayredhy and Tayreede, perhaps meaning Teriitahi, and said that the districts of Wyooreede and Attemono [Vaiari-iti and Attimaono], between Vaiari and Papara, belonged to her. Papara, Paea, and Punaauia were set down as belonging to Temarii, who controlled therefore the whole line of coast between Vaiari and Faaa. These districts contained more than one-fourth of the whole population then supposed to survive in Tahiti; forty-five hundred in the total of sixteen thousand.

Not only was Temarii the most powerful chief on the island, but Pomare had become, by his son's accession, a chief of the second order. He depended greatly on the favor of his son, the young Tu, who was, in 1797, supposed to be at least fifteen and perhaps seventeen years, old and who had been adopted by Temarii, his cousin, who was about ten years older than he. Adoption was rather stronger in the South Seas than the tie of natural parentage. Between his natural father, Pomare, and his adopted father, Temarii, the young Tu preferred the latter, and sooner or later everyone knew that Temarii would help Tu to emancipate himself and drive Pomare from the island. As the missionaries, following the English tradition, were Pomare's friends, they were in danger of sharing his fate.

Of this danger the missionaries had been warned before they had even landed. Old Manne Manne, as they called him, the high priest of Raiatea and Maraetaata, had tried to persuade them not to make common cause with Pomare, and brought the two Swedes to convince them that "Pomare never acted honorably by the English or any other after he had done with their services"; but the missionaries decided to follow the beaten path, assuming that Pomare and Tu were united in interest and could be courted and conciliated together. With this idea fixed in their minds, they landed at Matavai and put themselves in the hands of Pomare and his son.

The Duff sailed for England August 4, 1797, leaving the missionaries to be plundered or murdered by the rival factions, and they soon found that Pomare and Tu were far from being united. If they chose one, they must lose the other. Pomare chose as a brother, -- Towwa, as they spelt it, or hoa, or taeae, -- one of the missionaries, named Cover. Temarii chose another, named Main. These two missionaries went to Papara August 15, at Manne Manne's suggestion, to remonstrate against a human sacrifice which was to be made at the Marae of Tooarai. They fell into a most alarming danger, for they found Pomare, Tu and Terii navahoroa of Taiarapu, Pomare's two sons, with Temarii, and a swarm of people, greatly excited because, the night before, some of the Papara men had killed a man from Taiarapu. The two missionaries escaped as quickly as possible; but when, in the following February, Pomare, Tu, Temarii, Manne-manne, and their wives and following, came to Pare and remained there, escape was no longer possible. The missionaries found themselves more and more uncomfortable, and their situation became alarming in the month of March, 1798, when the ship Nautilus appeared and two of her crew deserted. The men went to Pare and were sheltered there. The captain of the Nautilus threatened to recover them, cost what it might; and four of the missionaries walked over to Pare to see Tu, Pomare and Temarii, and tell them that a refusal to surrender the men would be regarded as showing an evil intention against the missionaries.

They found Tu and Temarii at Pare, but went on to get Pomare to join them, when they were suddenly beset and stripped by some thirty natives, who took their clothes and treated them rather roughly, but at last let them go. They went on to Pomare's house and were received with the utmost humanity. Pomare went back with them to Tu, and insisted on the punishment of the offenders and the delivery of the seamen. Of course the attack had been made by men belonging to the interests of Tu and Temarii, and a few days afterwards war broke out. Pomare undertook to punish the offenders; two were killed, and the district of Pare took arms to revenge them. Tu joined his father and suppressed the resistance, so that the missionaries' clothes cost the lives of fifteen natives.

Such an affair was not calculated to make the missionaries popular, but it made them more than ever dependent on Pomare and Iddeah, his wife, who took pretty nearly complete control of all that the missionaries possessed. The helpless band were plundered by friends and enemies alike. Temarii was the only chief whom they did not charge with robbing or begging from them everything they had, but the relations between Temarii and Pomare were always threatening them with trouble. On August 24, two whaling-vessels, the Cornwall and Sally, of London, anchored in the bay, and most of the principal chiefs went on board. On the 30th, while the missionaries were at dinner, Pomare came in, and told them that a person had been blown up with gunpowder at the great house in Pare, and they were to go instantly with medicine to lend assistance. Two of them hastened away in a canoe to Pare, and ran to the place. There they found that the injured man was Temarii.

"At our arrival we were led to the bed of Temaree, called also Orepiah, and beheld such a spectacle as we had never before seen. Brother Broomhall began immediately to apply what he had prepared with a carnel's-hair brush over most part of his body. He was apparently more passive under the operation than we could conceive a man in his situation could be capable of. The night drawing on, we took leave of him by saying we would return in the morning with a fresh preparation. On the following morning... we were struck with much surprise at the appearance of the patient; he was literally daubed with something like a thick white paste. Upon our enquiry we found it to be the scrapings of yams. Both the chief and his wife seemed highly offended at Brother Broomhall's application the preceding evening, and they denied his doing anything more for him, as he had felt so much pain from what he had already done. It was said there was a curse put into the medicine by our God."

The poor missionaries were scared beyond expression, for they saw the imminent danger that some native, in a moment of superstitious anger, might offer them as a sacrifice to the injured native gods; but they returned bravely to their duty, until Tu's appearance proved too much for their nerves.

"In less than an hour [we] returned to the patient. Otoo and his wife were then riding in their usual style about the house with a train, or, more properly, a gang of the greatest villains on the island. They confronted that part of the house where we were assembled. Brother Broomhall and myself were at the foot of Orepiah's bed. I asked him to go out, and we would speak to the king. We went out, and I, with one of the usual salutations, addressed him. It was returned with a fallen countenance, without a word, which always denotes his wrath and often precedes the word taparahye -- that is, kill him -- for he thinks no more of sacrificing a man than cutting off a dog's neck. I saw plainly his executioners well knew his thoughts, and their eyes were fixed in a peculiar manner on me and on him, watching his motions. Otoo laid his hand on my shoulders and called one of his men to come to him."

Tu allowed them to go, and they started at once for Matavai, expecting never to reach it. "I thought the scene of March 26 was again about to be acted, only in a more tragic manner, inasmuch as the natives' suspicions then were small when compared with the present. At that time they suspected we had prevented Captains Bishop and Simpson, of the Nautilus, from bartering with them for musquets, but now they believed we had cursed the medicine that it might kill the patient, and that the greatest man on the island, he being closely allied with Otoo against his father and mother."

The suspicion that the missionaries were sent by Pomare to curse Temarii and cause his death was not only a natural but a reasonable one to the natives. Pomare was quite capable of it, and as far as the natives knew, the missionaries were Pomare's men. The accident itself was due to the English gunpowder, which had been as great a curse as every other English thing or thought had been; and perhaps it was fortunate for the missionaries that they had nothing to do with furnishing the powder. Temarii was well known to set great store on his armory. "His grand object was gunpowder; musquets he had a number of." The accident was due to his anxiety about the quality of some powder which he got from the whalers Cornwall and Sally on the 25th of August.

"Orepiah received his powder, to the amount of some pounds weight, out of one of the ships last here (Otoo, Pomere, &c., received a considerable quantity each, we hear, at the same time), and suspecting by the uncommon largeness of the grain that the Englishmen had put a deceit upon them by not giving them real powder, or having given them bad powder, Orepiah proposed to his attendants making an experiment. Accordingly a pistol was loaded and unthinkingly fired over the whole quantity of powder received, in the midst of a number of people. A spark of fire dropped from the pistol upon the powder that lay on the ground, and in a moment it blew up. The natives did not feel themselves hurt at first, but when the smoke was somewhat dispersed, observing their skin fouled with the powder, they began to rub their arms, &c., and found the skin to peel off under their fingers. Terrified at this, they instantly ran to a river near at hand and plunged themselves in. A despatch was immediately sent off to Pomare, who was at Matavai, acquainting him with the matter, and he made application to Brother Broomhall to go and give his assistance."

Under the stimulus of personal danger, the missionaries, in the course of a few days, learned much about island politics. Temarii lingered in great suffering till September 8, but the missionaries did not venture to visit him again, in spite of a message from Pomare asking them to administer something that would cure him without giving pain. The whole body of chiefs looked on, in consternation, while Temarii died.

"September 10th. The king [Tu], queen [Tetua], Pomere, Edea, Manne-manne, are to the westward, anxiously waiting the issue of the late calamitous visitation. We have reason to believe Orepiah's death would be the cause of great secret rejoicing to Pomere, Edea, and others, who seem to stand in much dread from the close union subsisting between Otoo and Orepiah; the latter being the uncle of the former, has acted as a kind of guardian to him during his youthful days. Though the wheels of political government are not so many in this as in our native island, yet they are more in number than any would conceive from the rude and barbarous state the nation is in. They have their plots and court intrigues, their parties and partisans, as well here as in England, and they are as important in their way as in the most refined court of Europe."

With better reasoning the natives looked at the missionaries as a kind of children, or idiots, incapable of understanding the simplest facts of island politics or society, and serving only as the unconscious tools of the Tu family. Day by day, the anxious party, studying their grammars at Matavai, learned more of the dangers which had menaced, and still threatened them, from Pare. The vital importance of Temarii's death to their interests gradually opened itself to their understandings.

"September 12.... The dead body, we hear, is to be carried in procession round the island, and much ceremony used on the occasion. This awful visitation is evidently to us a singular interposition of providence. What may be the consequences of it, time will unfold. There seemed to be such a rooted jealousy subsisting between Pomere, Edea, and the deceased, that we were every day in expectation of an open rupture. Orepiah seldom visited us; when he did. he always treated us civilly; though we have some ground to suppose he and Otoo were the principal agents in causing the four brethren to be stripped at Opare".

Temarii's body was carried, in the usual state, round the island to all his districts and duly mourned; and in the regular course prescribed by the island ceremonial, his head was secretly hidden in the cave at Papara, where, I believe, it still exists, marked by the gunpowder which caused Temarii's death. To the Papara people the disaster was hard to exaggerate, for the danger of their falling under the direct control of the Tu family, as Opunohu, Faaa, and Taiarapu had already done, was made imminent by the loss of their chief, who left no children and whose successor had no such connections or authority as the Temarii Ariifaataia had managed to acquire. To the rest of the island Temarii's death might be a blessing or a disaster, but could not escape being a crisis.

Before the mourning ceremonies were fully over the crisis began. For several days rumors came to the missionaries that Tu and his only remaining ally, Manne-manne, were sacrificing human victims, always the sign of some great emergency. Then the missionaries were told, on the night of November 16, that Tu was coming at daylight to attack the district. The trouble was caused by the funeral ceremony of Temarii. Pomare's orator or spokesman at Matavai, expressing the old hostility of Purionuu to Teva, sharpened by Temarii's notorious enmity, had said that Tu should not bring the body of Temarii to Matavai to be mourned, but should throw it into the sea. This was only the pretence for war. The true reason was that, after the death of Temarii, Tu and Manne-manne were obliged either to drive Pomare out of the island or submit to him. They had lost their support, and Pomare was too dangerous an intriguer for them to trust. Meanwhile Pomare had fled to the Paumotus, leaving Iddeah, his wife, to face the storm.

"Pomere's orator, who is a priest and also a rateera, or under-chief in a neighboring subdivision of the district, and who has been peculiarly familiar at brothers Eyre and Jefferson's, brought part of his property and put it under the care of brother Jefferson; from him we learnt this war would not affect us, it being against the natives of the district. He further told us that, as he and his countrymen were not able to make head against the king, they were constrained to fly for their lives and secrete themselves till the rage of Otoo shall be allayed.... Pomare is at the [Pau]-motoo, ignorant of the transactions of the day. We have more than once had occasion to notice a disunion between Otoo and his father, and a strong attachment between the former and the deceased chief Orepiah. The providential destruction of Orepiah, though it has deprived Otoo of a powerful ally, may have nothing lessened his disaffection to his father; indeed the occurrences of this day seem to be a proof it has not, or he would never have treated his father's friends as he has done for the imprudent speech of one or more persons. Edea is in Opare indisposed with the rheumatism; how far she approves of her son's conduct we know not. The chief of Taiaraboo (Otoo's younger brother) threatened some time ago to make war upon Otoo, and we have some reason to apprehend there is a league formed between him and his father, Pomere, and his uncle Vitua [Vae-tua], against Otoo."

The next day, November 18, brought a new budget of news to the missionaries at Matavai, where Tu and his followers were parading about their church, with occasional visits to ask for gifts.

"A little after morning service we heard that Otoo and Manne-manne had usurped the power over all the larger peninsula, and turned Pomere out from exercising authority in any part of the same. The districts of Opare, Tataha, Attahooroo, Papara, &c. (all the lands to the westward, and running round to the isthmus on the south), have declared for Otoo. The land of this district [Matavai], from the river before us to the eastern boundary, Otoo has given to Manne-manne, reserving the westernmost part for himself. If the districts on this side of the island [Teaharoa] to the isthmus shall refuse to acknowledge the authority of Otoo, we are informed war will be declared against them, and their submission extorted by force of arms. Something like this we expected, but did not imagine it would be put in execution so soon, since Temaree, who appeared to be at the head of the faction, was so suddenly cut off. Pomare's absence proved a favorable opportunity, and the indiscreet expressions of some of the inhabitants of this district respecting the corpse of Temaree, the cause of embracing it. Not long after our settling on the island we were told of there being two parties that were meditating the destruction of each other; hence arose the great eagerness of the chiefs to get muskets and ammunition into their hands from every vessel that has touched here; as also the desire of encouraging seamen to quit their ships and reside among them; knowing, by former experience, one musqueteer is sufficient to terrify many natives armed with clubs and spears. The Swedes and seamen are on Otoo and Manne-manne's side; so that, judging after the manner of men, and forming our conjectures from human reason and probability, we suppose the king and his party will carry all before them."

The same day Tetuani (Iddeah) arrived at Matavai, and a new scene began. Tetuanui was thirty years older than when she had succeeded in overthrowing Purea; and she, more than her husband Pomare, was the real intellect and energy of the party opposed to Papara. She and her brother Vaetua won all Pomare's victories, and upon them fell the task of resisting the Teva influence which controlled Tu. Pomare himself was not likely to return while the danger lasted; "It is said he is personally a great coward, and as Otoo and Manne-manne have the three Europeans with musquets (the very sight of which strikes terror in every breast) on their side, it is likely he will quietly submit to what is done till a more favorable opportunity occurs."

Tetuanui was not idle. On the 29th November she had made some bargain with Tu, ceding to him the authority he wanted, and obtaining from him the guaranty she needed for future good behavior. This guaranty was the life of old Manne-manne, Tu's last friend, the high-priest of Attahuru. He was murdered by Tetuanui's people, on his way from Matavai to Pare, and his body was carried to Tu's neighboring Marae of Taputapuatea. Tetuanui was in the missionaries' house when the news arrived, and at once "came to brother Eyre's door (she had a cartouch-box buckled round her waist; a musquet she had been seen with in her hand a little before was now laid aside) with a settled air of triumph on her brow; she shook hands in a friendly manner with the Swede, saying unto him: 'It is all over,' meaning the war, and retired immediately to the Point."

By this time the missionaries had learned more than any of their predecessors ever had known about island politics, and their final judgment on this affair, with their recapitulation of the whole story, was more rational than anything they had yet written.

"The conduct of Otoo, in consenting to the death of Manne-manne, at the time he was in close alliance with him, opens the character of the man in a conspicuous manner; and confirms us in a suspicion we have long entertained, but knew not how to account for, concerning the stripping of brothers Broomhall, Jefferson, Main, and W. Puckey, at Opare. When that circumstance took place we seemed assured it was done by the king's [Tu's] authority, but when Otoo afterwards joined his father in punishing the poor people for the same, we could not readily reconcile his authorizing the action, and then destroying those that did it. But we have seen so much of him since, that we believe he is capable of comitting any wickedness the devil, his carnal mind, and bloodthirsty followers may excite him to, if God did not restrain him; we therefore think the true cause of that event was this: Tema-ree, the foster-father of Tu, was in close connection with him, and clearly appeared to be meditating some great blow by which they would exclude every other person from having authority on the island but themselves and followers. To effect this they were extremely desirous to get into their hand musquets and ammunition. When the bark Nautilus arrived, finding that she had a large quantity of these articles on board, but that they were deterred from obtaining them through our interference, they were offended, and determined to be revenged. Accordingly, when the Nautilus arrived the second time, and the two seamen escaped from her and took refuge with Otoo, and the four brethren were despatched with an endeavor to recover them, the king, thinking it a favorable opportunity to execute his revenge upon the society, secretly gave orders for their being plundered. Otoo and Temaree, though powerful, were not sufficiently strong at the time to oppose Pomare, who showed displeasure at what was done; and though no doubt he was acquainted with the true authors of the action yet from prudent motives, it may be, he vented his anger upon the instruments, rather than the movers of them; while Otoo and Temaree, to hide their crime, joined Pomare in so doing. "

The missionaries escaped marvelously, at the cost of a stripping and a little terror. The unfortunate natives who stripped them paid with their lives for the offence. Temarii lost his life also, and his scheme for restoring the supremacy of Papara failed. Papara, as every one might foresee, must be the sacrifice once more to the ambition of the Purionuu chiefs. Manne-manne was another victim. Pomare gained nothing, for he had nothing to gain, but had to sacrifice a part of his possessions. The only winner in this tragic game was the worst and most bloodthirsty of all -- Tu, the first Christian king.

CHAPTER XIV

Meanwhile Europe had totally lost its first keen interest in Tahiti. Like an old fashion, the South Seas fell into the hands of unfashionable people such as missionaries and whaling-captains; the glamour vanished, and the worn-out excitement faded away. When Cook returned from his second voyage, he brought with him a young native from Raiatea named Omai, and rather apologetically explained that he was not a fair specimen of the islanders either in birth or appearance. He seemed surprised to find that this specimen of "the middling class of people" proved to be a social success in London. "Soon after his arrival the Earl of Sandwich the first Lord of the Admiralty, introduced him to his Majesty at Kew, when he met with a most gracious reception, and imbibed the strongest impression of duty and gratitude to that great and amiable prince, which I am persuaded he will preserve to the latest moment of his life". He remained two years in England, 1775-1776, "caressed by many of the principal nobility" and attained even the great distinction of approval from Doctor Johnson as was recorded by Boswell, whose sense of humor seems to have been in no way stirred by the characteristic remarks of Johnson on the subject of polite manners in England and elsewhere.

"He (Johnson) had been in company with Omai, a native of one of the South Sea Islands, after he had been some time in this country. He was struck with the elegance of his behavior, and accounted for it thus: 'Sir, he had passed his time while in England only in the best company, so that all that he had acquired of our manners was genteel'".

One would like to have Omai's impression of Johnson's manners, but Omai had no Boswell, and left no memoirs, although he left something as good, for his portrait was painted by Sir Joshua Reynolds, and, no doubt, is valued more highly now than ever Omai was in his native island, even when Cook brought him back there in 1777, loaded with gifts, which were probably soon appropriated by his chiefs or neighbors. A few years afterwards, in 1785, before Omai had wholly passed from memory, the poet Cowper devoted to him a page or two in the first book of "The Task", which bore the odd title of "The Sofa". Whether it was that Cowper's melancholia caused him to see things as they are, or whether years had brought already a disillusionment that was to make rapid progress in European thought, certainly the lines in the "Sofa" contained more truth if not more poetry than anything which had been said till then on the subject of the South Seas:

"Thee, gentle savage, whom no love of thee

Or thine, but curiosity, perhaps,

Or else vain glory, prompted us to draw

Forth from thy native bowers, to show thee here

With what superior skill we can abuse

The gifts of Providence, and squander life.

.... Duly every morn

Thou climbst the mountain top, with eager eye
Exploring far and wide the watery waste
For sight of ship from England. Every speck
Seen in the dim horizon turns thee pale
With conflict of contending hopes and fears.
But comes at last the dull and dusky eve,
And sends thee to thy cabin, well prepared
To dream all night of what the day denied.
Alas! expect it not! We found no bait
To tempt us in thy country. Doing good,
Disinterested good, is not our trade.
We travel far, 'tis true, but not for nought;
And must be bribed to compass earth again
By other hopes and richer fruits than yours".

Cowper did his country injustice. The London Missionary Society was formed in 1795 for no other object than to do disinterested good, and selected the South Seas for its first field of operations. The missionary ship "Duff" set sail from England in August, 1796, and reached Tahiti in March, 1797.

Thirty years had elapsed between the coming of Captain Wallis in the Dolphin and the coming of the missionaries in the Duff. Little was left of all that had charmed the discoverers. In these thirty years Europe had also passed through the experience of centuries; the dreams of Rousseau and the ideals of nature were already as far away as the kingdom of heaven. In 1797 the philosophers were dead; the guillotine had disposed of the innate virtues of the human heart; and war had swept away most of the landmarks of old Europe, with much of its old population; but the wreck of society that had occurred in Europe was not to be compared with the wreck of our world in the South Seas. When England and France began to show us the advantages of their civilization, we were, as races then went, a great people. Hawaii, Tahiti, the Marquesas, Tonga, Samoa, and New Zealand made a respectable figure on the earth's surface, and contained a population of no small size, better fitted than any other possible community for the conditions in which they lived. Tahiti, being first to come into close contact with, the foreigners, was first to suffer. The people, who numbered, according to Cook, two hundred thousand in 1767, numbered less than twenty thousand in 1797, according to the missionaries, and only about five thousand in 1803. This frightful mortality has been often doubted, because Europeans have naturally shrunk from admitting the horrors of their own work, but no one doubts it who belongs to the native race. Tahiti did not stand alone in misery. What happened there happened everywhere, not only in the great groups of high islands, like Hawaii, with three or four hundred thousand people, but in little coral atolls which could support only a few score. Moerenhout, who was the most familiar of all travellers with the islands in our part of the ocean, told the same story about all. He was in the Austral group in 1834. At Raivavae he found ninety or a hundred natives rapidly dying, where fully twelve hundred had been living only twelve or fourteen years before. At Tubuaihe found less than two hundred people among the ruins of houses, temples and tombs. At Rurutu and Rimitara, where a thousand or twelve hundred people had occupied each, hardly two hundred were left, and while nearly all the men had died at Rimitara, nearly all the women had been swept away at Rurutu. The story of the Easter Islanders is famous. That of the Marquesas is almost as pathetic as that of Tahiti or Hawaii. Everywhere the Polynesian perished, and to him it mattered little whether he died of some new disease, or from some new weapon, like the musket, or from the misgovernment caused by foreign intervention.

No doubt the new diseases were the most fatal. Almost all of them took some form of fever, and comparatively harmless epidemics, like measles, became frightfully fatal when the native, to allay the fever, insisted on bathing in cold water. Dysenteries and ordinary colds, which the people were too ignorant and too indolent to nurse, took the proportion of plagues. For forty generations these people had been isolated in this ocean, as though they were in a modern sanata-rium, protected from contact with new forms of disease, and living on vegetables and fish. The virulent diseases which had been developed among the struggling masses of Asia and Europe found a rich field for destruction when they were brought to the South Seas. Just as such pests as the lantana, the mimosa or sensitive plant, and the guavahave overrun many of the islands, where the field for them was open, so diseases ran through the people.

For this, perhaps, the foreigners were not wholly responsible, although their civilization certainly was; but for the political misery the foreigner was wholly to blame, and for the social and moral degradation he was the active cause. No doubt the ancient society of Tahiti had plenty of vices, and was a sort of Paris in its refinements of wickedness; but these had not prevented the islanders from leading as happy lives as had ever been known among men. They were like children in their morality and their thoughtlessness, but they flourished and multiplied. The Europeans came, and not only upset all their moral ideas, but also their whole political system. In old times, whenever a single chief became intolerably arrogant or threatened to destroy the rest, the others united to overthrow him. All the wars that are remembered in island tradition were caused by the overweening pride, violence or ambition of the great chiefs or districts, and ended in restoring the balance. The English came just at the moment when one of these revolutions occurred. The whole island had united to punish the chiefess of Papara for outrageous disregard of the courtesies which took the place of international law between great chiefs. They had punished Purea, had taken away the symbol of sovereignty she had assumed for her son, and had given it for safe-keeping to the chief of Paea. They had recognized the chief of Pare Arue as entitled to wear the Maro-ura, which Purea had denied him by insulting his wife. Then the chief of Paea had tried to imitate Purea and assert supreme authority, only to be in his turn defeated and killed. Probably Tu would have never attempted to imitate Tutaha and Purea if the English had not insisted on treating him as king of the whole island. He was one of the weakest of the chiefs and enjoyed little consideration as far as his military power was concerned. The other chiefs would have easily kept him in his place if the English had not constantly supported him and restored his strength when he was overthrown. English interference alone prolonged his ambition and caused the constant wars which gave no chance for the people to recover from their losses.

Pomare could gain his object in no other way than by destroying one after another the whole of the old chiefly class. As long as one of them survived he was sure to be the champion of the great body of islanders who detested the tyranny of a single ruler, and knew what such a tyranny meant for them. If their legends show nothing else, they show that the natives knew much more about tyranny, and had much more reason to dread it, than the English or the French had known for many centuries; and against such a despotism as Europe could not realize, their tribal system, with its chiefs, was their only protection. They clung to it, and Pomare had no choice but to succumb, or to destroy it. He was a consummate politician, for the art of politics was the life of the chiefly class, and every chief knew by instinct and by close personal contact the character and thought of every other chief on the island. Pomare knew that what he was trying to do could be done only by wholesale destruction, and that, in order to do it, he must depend on outsiders; white men or Raiateans or savages from the Paumotus. The missionaries knew it also, for Pomare made no secret of it, and they recorded it as though it did not concern them.

"In a conversation a brother had with Pomere [in October, 1800], the chief gave him to understand that there is a probability of war upon the island, but not directly. He did not seem to know who were his friends, or who his foes, but acknowledged the general desire of the people is a suppression of a monarchical form of government, and the reestablishment of independency in each district. It was observed to him that the arbitrary proceedings of Otoo were probably the cause of the present discontent. He did not deny it. Pomere wished much for a ship of war to arrive, which he supposed, by an interference in his favor, would restore tranquillity and confirm his and his son's authority. Or if a number of Englishmen like ourselves were to join us, and continue their residence among them in the manner we have done, he said he was sure there would be no war."

The missionaries' journals were as full of such evidence as the journals of Cook, Bligh, and Vancouver had been. All told how desperately the unfortunate people struggled against the English policy of creating and supporting a tyranny. The brutality and violence of Tu made him equally hated by his own people of Pare and by the Teva districts. I give a few such extracts to show what the missionaries saw and what they did.

"October 16 [1799].... Heard that five human sacrifices have, within a few days, been brought over from Eimeo to this island; also that many of the inhabitants of Opare (of the poorest sort) have fled to the mountains to avoid being seized for human sacrifices, as Otoo and Pomere are looking out for what they deem fit objects for that purpose.... It appears that these things are preparations for the purposed war, and that Pomere is doing what other blind heathens have done before him, laboring to bribe his idol-god to be propitious to him, and to forsake the district of Attahooroo.

"October 17. It is said the cause of the present war with Attahooroo is that the inhabitants of that district have resented the tyrannical and oppressive conduct of the chiefs, who exercise with an high hand their authority over those subject to their power.

"January 1, 1800. At one in the afternoon Otoo, Pomere and Edea assembled before brother Eyre's apartment, and the brethren presented unto each a musket and one four-pound cartridge."

[Letter to the. Rev. John Love, for the directors of the Missionary Society, January 14, 1800J. -- "This island is at present in a state of tranquility, but we fear ere long it will be involved in war, as a great disagreement is subsisting between Otoo, Pomere, &c., and the district of Attahooroo, one of the most powerful divisions of the island. From the Eliza has been landed on Pomere's account (without any interference of ours) one eighteen-pound carronade, two swivels, several muskets, and a great deal of ammunition."

"May 21. Hear there are commotions among the lower classes of natives against Pomere, chiefly on account of his tyrannical conduct (it is said) in frequently plundering them of their little property.

"May 23. Rumors of war still continue. It is reported that the commonalty are much moved against the principal chiefs, and are wanting to root them up altogether, and to restore the ancient form of government to the island: that is, every district to be subject to its own chief, without the acknowledgment of a superior over him. Our present situation appears very dangerous, but the Lord sitteth above the flood, and our times are in his hands. The depredations and wanton-ness practiced by Otoo's people upon the commonalty are said to be among the causes for the desire of a change of government....

"January 21,1801. War is still the subject of conversation around us; the common people harboring destructive thoughts against Pomere and all his family....

"January 31.... It is surprising what havock disease has made since we have been on the island [March, 1797]. Matavai is almost depopulated in comparison to what it once was, according to the accounts given by the natives; and not only this district but the whole island....

"February 2. Brothers Eyre and Henry, who were to-day out about the district, visiting the natives, bring a melancholy report of the appearances of things. The country very scantily peopled; the low lands overrun with long grass and underwoods which form swamps, stop the circulation of air, and tend much to the unhealthiness of the inhabitants; add to which the spirit of disaffection that is prevailing among the lower classes against Pomere and Otoo.

"March 6. This day four years we arrived at Otaheite, and have hitherto been preserved in a very kind and gracious manner. At present we see no good arising from our residence among the Otaheitans.

"June 26. A vessel came in sight.... The vessel proved to be His Majesty's armed ship the Porpoise, Lieutenant Scott commander, from Port Jackson [Sydney]. The commander delivered to us, from Governor King, a letter on His Majesty's service, [and] a letter to Pomere.

"June 30. [Note]. By intelligence that we have received, it seems that the arrival of the Porpoise is a very providential interference, as the affairs of this country were brought to such a crisis that a few days, if not hours, would have either dethroned Otoo or established him in his authority; this could not have been done without much bloodshed, the effusion of which we hope is now stopped, and Otoo and family will be permitted to retain quiet possession of their dignity. The Lord does all things well.

"July 13.... Pomere again spoke about our engaging in war for him. He said the island was in a very disaffected state towards him; that a relation of his, the chief of Bola-bola, was in a dangerous situation; that his country was involved in war, himself wounded, and if he was to be overcome, the commonalty of Otaheite would rise upon him and us, and kill us all. Again we told him we would have nothing to do with war. Captain Wilson promised him three or four musquets and that he would also visit Bola-bola, and leave a musquet or two for his use. With this Pomere appeared satisfied."

These notes, which extend over eighteen months, describe the whole experience of the missionaries. They were frank and simple-minded, and made no secret of their situation towards Otoo, which is clearly described in a letter they wrote to the commander of a captured Spanish ship which put into Matavai Bay, February 1, 1799:

"Our situation is so critical among these people that we find it difficult so to carry ourselves as not to give offence to one or the other. Otoo, the king, is solicitous to have a musquet from the ship through our hands. We find it necessary for us, in order to preserve peace, to solicit you to grant us a musquet, if you can possibly spare one, for Otoo; and any return in our power to make, or a draft upon our brethren in England, for the value of the same, we will gladly give."

To preserve peace the missionaries did some very curious things which suggest, as they hinted, that they were glad to see the natives fighting together.

"August 20 [1800].... We hear great preparations are making, whether for war or peace is to be determined in a short time by some heathenish divination. If it should prove for war, those who are eager for blood seem determined to glut themselves. We rejoice that the Lord of Hosts is the God of the heathen as well as the Captain of the armies of Israel; and while the potsherds of the earth are dashing themselves to pieces one against the other, they are but fulfilling his determinate counsels and foreknowledge."

This Calvinistic or fatalistic view of the heathen justified or excused every possible action on all sides of every question, but the close neighborhood of contrary ideas was sometimes still more curious in the missionary records.

"June 23 [1801], Agreed that to-morrow be sanctified as a fast unto the Lord to supplicate him in a peculiar manner at this juncture in behalf of the inhabitants of the island; that he would be graciously pleased to keep them in peace among themselves, to open the door for the preaching and success of his gospel among them, to have mercy upon us, and help us to be able ministers and good stewards of the word of his grace.

"June 25. Mr. Broomhall, William Smith (late cooper of the Eliza), and two natives came from Opare with orders from Pomere to take out of the storeroom some iron rods, which are to be cut into small pieces and used as slugs or cannister shot for the swivel and car-ronade that Pomare has taken with him. They accordingly took out four nail-rods for the purpose."

Alternately praying for peace and helping Pomare and Tu to make war, the missionaries innocently hastened the destruction of the natives, and encouraged the establishment of a tyranny impossible for me to describe. Pomare was vicious and cruel, treacherous and violent beyond the old code of chiefly morals, but Pomare was an angel compared with his son Tu. I do not care to enter on the chapter of his personal vices, all which were as notorious to the missionaries as to the natives, but as he grew older -- in 1800 he was eighteen or twenty years of age -- and as he gained power, he developed a character such as the natives did not recognize as theirs, but ascribed to his savage Paumotu ancestry. The missionaries spoke constantly of the intense hatred caused by his treatment of the common people in his own districts of Pare Arue and Matavai: but if the missionaries, who held themselves aloof from other chiefs for fear of offending Pomare, had taken the trouble to inquire into the true nature of their situation, they would have found that the hatred of Tu was not confined to the commonalty or to the poor wretches reserved for human sacrifice. No doubt Tu carried human sacrifices, in his constant wars, to a point such as terrified beyond all previous experience the common people, whose numbers were so much diminished that three persons, taken for sacrifice, counted relatively as fifty or a hundred would have done a generation before; but even with this terror on their minds, and with the constant robbery of their property which Tu practised, the common people neither hated nor feared Tu more than he was hated and feared by their superiors and their local chiefs.

Already Pomare had succeeded in extinguishing the Vehiatuas of Taiarapu, and seizing that important district for his son. He had equally set aside the Ahurai family. He had established his own power in Eimeo, over the northern portion of the island. The old Teva districts and Hitiaa alone maintained an attitude of independence, and although Temarii Ariifaataia was dead the people of Attahuru, or Paea, with whom the whole population of the coast from Faaa to the isthmus were engaged, offered resistance that Pomare and Tu were afraid to defy without English aid. In the meanwhile, Tu threw aside all regard for the old courtesies of society, and terrified the chiefs as much as he terrified the mean people. Had they been the outcast class from which human victims were generally taken, the chiefs could hardly have been treated with more disrespect.

One or two such cases, showing the terror which Tu inspired among the chiefs, came under the notice of the missionaries. One related to members of Tu's own family:

"March 5 [1799].... The king and queen often about our habitations. Otoo very childish and brutish, and his attendants imitators of him.

"March 6.... A great concourse of natives about us, who are passing their time in eating, drinking, wrestling, drum-beating, singing, hallooing, throwing their arms and legs about in a frantic manner, and such like revellings. This assembly is owing to a marriage ceremony that is about to be performed between a chief of Oryatea [Raiatea], named Matte-ah, and a young woman, the daughter of the deceased chief of this district, named Mahei-annoo. She and Matte-ah are both branches of Pomere's family, and chiefs by birth....

"March 12.... Matte-ah aud Mahei-annoo, &c., went to the four brethren's habitation, carrying with them a great part of their property and prayed the brethren to take the same under their care, having just heard that Otoo had taken offence at the family, and had threatened to plunder and kill some of them. They appeared to be much agitated and distressed in mind. The brethren received their effects into their custody, and they returned to their dwelling declaring they would all die together. Their speech and looks were very affecting. Otoo's anger against the family, it is said, is because, when Matte-ah and Mahei-annoo were united, ... they went into the king's morai, which no one but himself is permitted to do. But this the family declares is false, that they kept to their own morai, and entered not into that of the king's. When we reflect upon the tyrannical disposition of Otoo, and the barbarous state of the natives, our peaceable situation in the midst of them is truly marvellous in our eyes."

On this occasion, as on most others where the victims received warning in time to prepare, Otoo denied the report, and the threatened chiefs were allowed to live. The full meaning of the incident appears in a later entry in the missionaries' journal.

"October 21 [1800].... Heard of the death of Mahei-annoo, the wife of Matte-ah. Her disorder was the evil in her neck, by which the passage of her throat was so destroyed as to prevent her receiving food. About three days before she died she was delivered of a dead child. She was in a district on the south side of the island called Puppe-haare, to which place she was taken the latter end of last month.... She was a young woman of good sense, considering her education, and in a great measure free from that levity which characterizes the inhabitants of this island."...

The person whom Otoo had thus terrified was no other than the beautiful Maheanuu of Papeari (Puppe-haare), the head of island society, as much the social superior of Tu as Tu was, by virtue of his English arms, the political superior over Matavai. To the natives, and especially to the Tevas, Tu in threatening to kill her and her husband was guilty of every atrocity known to the island code of morals and manners. Napoleon did not so much shock Europe by killing the Due d'Enghien as Tu would have shocked Tahiti by treachery to the Maheanuu and her husband.

The next example of the terror inspired by Tu among the greatest chiefs was in the case of Teohu, chief of Hitiaa, who came in March, 1801, to Matavai, with all his double canoes, in full chiefly state, with two human sacrifices, to make a treaty with Pomare and Tu. After the ceremony was over, and Pomare had returned to Pare, the missionaries recorded:

"April 15. During the night a woman came from Opare by water and brought Teohu and party word that it was Pomere's intention to kill him. This information threw them into a consternation, and the fighting men instantly armed, and placed themselves round the old chief as a guard. It appears that the woman who brought the intelligence is one of Teohu's party, and had mingled herself with Pomere's whence she gained her information. That Pomere will kill him if he can, there is perhaps but little reason to doubt, and Teohu is himself apprehensive of it, and much afraid, though Pomere carries himself with a great deal of apparent kindness towards him, and has even gone so far as to make him a present of a musket."

The chiefess of Papeari and the chief of Hitiaa were personages of great dignity, but the chief of Papara held more real power than them all, including Pomare and Tu. In order to establish his superior power, Tu could not avoid the necessity of destroying the Papara family, and putting one of the Pare Arue family in the chiefery of Papara. Accordingly, after the death of Temarii Ariifaataia, no chief of Papara was ever seen at Matavai. The missionaries, who mentioned every one else, never mentioned his name, or seemed aware that Temarii had a successor. They knew that Papara and Paea were in chronic revolt against Tu, but they did not care to know who led the revolt. They were satisfied to give Tu muskets and gunpowder to conquer Papara and destroy its chiefs without their knowing their own victim.

CHAPTER XV

I have succeeded in following, after a fashion, the careers of the Papara chiefs until the death of Ariifaataia in September 1798, so that Amo and Purea and even Ariifaataia himself have a kind of reality to me, but as I come to the dark ages of our history, between 1800 and 1815, I find a want of records and traditions that shows how narrowly our family must have escaped the fate of almost every other chiefly race. The successor to Ariifaataia as chief at Papara could not be a descendant of Amo or Purea or Ariifaataia. Their line was extinct. The line of succession had to go back to Amo's younger brother Manea -- who had washed away Purea's blood-feud at Mahai-atea, which is all I know about him. He was probably dead in 1798, but, even if alive, he must have been an old man, between seventy and eighty; and in Tahiti old men were not much regarded. He had a son, Teuraiterai, born probably about 1750, who married Tetau i Ravea, and had several children. The oldest son, Taura atua i Patea, afterwards known as Tati, who died in 1854, supposed himself then to be eighty years old. He remembered having seen Cook, when a child, and as Cook's last voyage was in 1777, the young Taura atua could hardly have been born later than 1774. He had a brother, Opuhara, born probably a year or two later.

When Ariifaataia died in 1798, Taura atua must have been about twenty-four, or twenty-five, years old. He was then unmarried. As far as I know, his relations with Tu were friendly and he succeeded quietly to the chiefery, but I can learn nothing about his doings. He was always a wise and peaceful man, who gained his objects by diplomacy rather than by force, and preferred alliance with the Pomares rather than war.

During the next ten or fifteen years the books and printed records contain hardly a mention of the chief of Papara. Even in the great war of 1802, the war about the God Oro, provoked by Pomare, no allusion is made to Papara or its chief. A single allusion to a Temarre occurs in December 1803, but nothing more.

Vairatoa, the first Pomare, died suddenly, Sept. 3, 1803, about sixty years old, and his son Otoo, the second Pomare, went to Eimeo or Moorea, in the middle of 1804, where he remained till 1806. In January of that year he returned, and in June 1807, he committed an act which made the people of Tahiti, and particularly the whole Teva clan, thenceforward deadly and irreconcileable enemies to the Pomares and all their friends and faiths, as well as to missionaries, Christianity and the English interest, until the final catastrophe of 1815. Far later and even down to this day, the memory of Otoo's treachery and cruelty in 1807 has survived among the people, and perhaps still more among the chiefs.

From day to day the missionaries recorded what they saw or heard, with very little attempt at explanation, and no apparent suspicion that they were in any way parties to the events they deplored:

"Monday. 11 June 1807. The man mentioned as being inspired continues to say that the God Oro is angry and that there must be war. The principal offence, we understand, is that the people of Attahuru have taken some of the bones of the chief Mateha who was killed by them the last war at Taearabu, and made fish-hooks of them, which has been done by way of contempt to the King, as he was a relative to Pomare's family. There are several other things which have displeased the king. Also the people of Taearabu have given some offence possibly by their not wholly leaving the land given to Oro, which the king had desired should not be inhabited. The king and the people in general about us are busily employed in cleaning their muskets and preparing themselves for war, and seem much delighted with the certainty of its taking place.

"Friday. 22. A messenger from Attahuru or Pape Ere brought to the King, who happened to be at our house at the time, a tara aehara, or atonement. It consisted of a branch of plantain, a bunch of red feathers, and a sucking-pig. It is said that it was sent on account of Pepere who is very ill at Attahuru. The king ordered it to be taken to his mother. It is supposed an expedition against Attahuru is in agitation, and that it will take place when certain religious ceremonies are performed.

"Monday 25. Three of the bodies of the slain at Attahuru were brought up during the night; these and the two brought here yesterday afternoon are sent forward to Taearabu to be deposed in the Marae where the God Orois. It is reported that eight are killed altogether... In the course of the day some people came from Attahuru, and they report that Pomare and his people are encamped in Attahuru, and that all the Attahuruans are fled to their Pare. All the houses and plantations have been destroyed by Pomare's party, and much spoil was taken, the Attahuruans not having time to take it with them. Cloth and other things are sent up today in great quantities to the districts of Pare and Matavae.

"Tuesday (?) July 2. Pomare sent us a note signifying that the Attahuruans are entirely subdued and destroyed; that Tata-ru, Poeno, etc., are among the slain; and requesting us to send him some paper to make cartridges, and two bottles of rum. A little of the former was sent him, but the latter was denied; a note also was sent him requesting him not to proceed in destroying harmless women and children. Held our missionary prayer-meeting at the usual time. In the afternoon brothers Elder and Wilson went down towards Attahuru to see whether they can do anything to save those fugitives that are said to be in the mountains. Brother Nott also went down to Pare intending to conduct hither Te Towha, a chief of Attahuru who escaped the late slaughter by running to the mountains, and is supposed to be now in the valley of Hautana. Pomare has promised that on account of his sister (who is the wife of Pare) he shall be spared; at the same time it is supposed that Pomare would be glad of his death.

"Wednesday, 3... In the evening the brethren returned. Brother Nott could not find Te Towha; he is hiding himself somewhere in the mountains. Brothers Elder and Wilson proceeded to Pomare's camp; but when they got there he was on the point of sailing for Papara where most of his followers had gone before...

Pomare was standing by the dead bodies on the seaside, giving orders to the people and waiting till all the carcasses of the slain should be put on board canoes to send to the great Marae at Taearabu. The brethren saw only about thirty; the rest had been previously sent away for Taearabu; those they saw were cut and mangled in a shocking manner. The number of the slain is not easily ascertained; the brethren conjecture they might not exceed one hundred. The district of Attahuru presents a horrid scene of ruin and devastation. Pomare appeared as if he was conscious of acting wrong, but was not for entering into conversation with the brethren. They requested him not to proceed in killing the women and children, and entreated him to spare the Attahuruans that are in the mountains: this he promised to do."

Here ends the Missionary Diary. The next letter, dated Nov. 12, 1808, announces their departure from the island in company with Pomare himself, driven away by the universal outbreak caused by Pomare's massacres of June. Other such massacres had occurred, but this was the most atrocious, and the missionaries themselves did not know the full atrocity of the act. Ellis's abstract contains no more facts than the Diary furnished him. Moerenhaut continues the story from the point where the missionaries broke off:

"After having massacred all whom they had surprised [in Attahuru], after having burned the houses, they went on to Papara, where Tati, who is still living [1837] was chief; but fortunately a man who had escaped from the carnage of Punaauia came to warn the inhabitants of Papara, so that they had time, not to unite in defence, but to fly. Nevertheless, in that infernal night and the day following, a great number of persons perished, especially old men, women and children; and among the victims were the widow and children of Aripaia [Ariifaataia], Amo's son, who, surprised the next evening near Taiarapu, were pitilessly massacred with all their attendants. Tati, and some of his warriors, succeeded in reaching a fort called Papeharoro at Mairepehe; but they were too few to maintain themselves there, and were forced to take refuge in the most inaccessible parts of the high mountains, from whence this chief succeeded in getting to a canoe which some of his faithful followers procured for him, arid kept ready on the shore, at the peril of their lives. With him were his brother and his young son whom he had himself carried in his arms during all this time of fatigues and dangers."

Our tradition of the massacre is somewhat different and more picturesque, for it carries the murders back to the old feud of Purea and Pomare's mother Tetuanui reiaite, and the scene on the beach at Mahaiatea in 1768. Whether Tetuanui, whom the English called Iddeah, Idia, and the like, was still living in 1807 is unknown to me; but she was alive as late as 1803 when her husband Pornare Vairatoa died, and the feud lived with her. The island custom required that the chiefs children should be brought up not with their parents but with their nurses, for the etiquette of the island was more than royal; it was hereditary and sacred, and the nurses had a religious right to the charge of the children. In 1807 the children were living with their household at Vaiari.

Pomare sent out men from Tarahoi to kill them in order to atone for the blood of Terii Vaetua and Tetuanui reiaite that had been spilt for the insult offered by Purea. The revenge resulted in the murder of two of Tati's sisters and three cousins, but Tati with his cousin Ariipaea, commonly known as Veve, escaped across the mountains to Mahaena on the east coast where they were pursued by the murderers. The chief of Mahaena was a distant relation, and had an old tie of hospitality to requite. He took the two young men under his protection, and defied Pomare. The blood-feud had been wiped away by Manea as far as he or his descendents were concerned, and Pomare did not care for the death of Tati so much as for that of his cousin; but seeing that he could not gain his object, he invited the two to Pare, guaranteeing their safety. They went to Pare, but fearing treachery escaped from there to Borabora where they remained for the next few years. Opuhara was saved by his servants who took him to Papara where he was beyond Pomare's reach.

According to our tradition the Hiva at Papara would not recall Tati. The outrage of June, 1807, had exhausted the last remnants of patience in the islanders, and this time the whole island rose, determined to make clean work of Pomare and all his surroundings. For this purpose they needed a warrior, and as a warrior Opuhara had no superior. So Opuhara became chief of Papara, and soon afterward head chief of the island; for he and his army advanced to Papenoo in 1808, and there, on December 22, Pomare attacked them, and was totally defeated. Pomare and his household, and the whole missionary establishment, without waiting for further notice, abandoned the island, and fled to Eimeo. During the next seven years, Opuhara was the chief personage in Tahiti.

"Upufara", says Ellis, the historian of the missionaries, "was an intelligent and interesting man." Although he was the last hero of Paganism and the chief opponent of the missionaries, the missionaries always spoke well of him, and belived that he meant them no personal harm. Of Pomare, on the contrary, they spoke with horror. I have already quoted enough of their language on that subject, and neither the manners nor the morals of the king were such as one cares to insist upon; but as a politician Pomare offered an example fully as bad as that which he set for private morality. He had never at any time a large following of his own; and outside of his own Pare Arue he had none. More and more his wars came to be carried on by foreign ruffians, either from the Paumotus, or such as Peter Haggerstein, the Swede, who was regarded by all other Europeans, whether missionaries or traders, as one of the most thorough villains unhung. At Eimeo his friends were Paumotuans, Boraborans, Raiateans, missionaries, or outcasts. He lived on what he could beg from European ships or from the missionaries. Even the Raiateans, Boraborans and missionaries at last deserted him. The missionary journal shews that they had long regarded their work as a failure; and, after identifying themselves with Pomare, in spite of emphatic warnings, no other result was possible. So the missionaries, leaving only Mr Nott at Eimeo, sailed away to Port Jackson, or Botany Bay, where the city of Sydney now stands, not daring to accept the proffered protection of the Tahiti chiefs because they could not separate themselves, in the minds of the common people, from Pomare and his interests.

What little we know of Papara and Opuhara during the next seven years, from December, 1808, to November, 1815, comes chiefly from Moerenhout, who must have got it from Tati. What we know of Pomare comes chiefly from the missionary histories. The person whose doings are most difficult to follow is Tati himself. We know that he went to Borabora, having married Tehea, who belonged to one of the three chiefly families of that island. We know, too, that Pomare, not long afterwards, contracted to marry, as his second wife, the elder daughter of Tamatoa, chief of Raiatea; but that the younger daughter, Terito, managed to get first to Eimeo, and was taken by Pomare as queen, in spite of the contract with her elder sister, who arrived only after Terito was fairly installed. The violation of faith was so flagrant that Pomare left to the elder sister the official title of queen, -- Pomare vahine, -- and queen she remained all her life, as far as concerned political energy, courage and control. Tamatoa came up to the marriage with his daughter. The wedding party seems to have been assembling at Eimeo, November 8,1811, when Pomare wrote to the missionaries in New South Wales describing his situation.

"Taheite is in peace", he said; "it is not a very good peace; perhaps it will not be good until there is war again; however there is peace, and we remain in quietness. I came here to Eimeo July the 8th to get timber for canoes, and dwell at Eimeo... Tapoa and party are here at Eimeo, and also the chiefs of Ulitea [Raiatea]. Tamatoa and Pomare vahene are at Huaheine; they only remain of the chiefs. They are to come in Captain Walker's vessel; perhaps they will not come for some time yet. Tapoa and party came in Captain Campbell's vessel. They arrived here at Eimeo September 27th. They brought a good number of men with them, 288."

Tati was one of Tapoa's party, which arrived on September 27th, and numbered nearly three hundred. Other parties from the leeward numbered 461 more, so that Pomare had at Eimeo a formidable army.

"They also are come", he continued, "to engage in the war. I shall send them back again; there shall be no war; there is peace and not war." His reasons for sending them home, he did not give; but he was certainly not yet ready for another war. He had still to work out his plan of carrying over his whole party to open Christianity; a plan which, as his letters show, must have been in his mind for years. Tamatoa arrived soon afterwards, and Pomare then tried to persuade him and the other chiefs from the leeward islands to declare themselves Christians. He came on the 18th July, 1812, to announce his own decision to the missionaries, and shortly afterwards, on invitation from his old district of Pare Arue, he returned to Tahiti, where he was allowed to remain for two years, as an avowed Christian, unmolested by his old enemies.

At the same time, Tati came home and was received again at Papara. Pomare set up his residence at Pare Arue as a Christian chief August 13, 1812, and kept up a correspondence with the missionaries at Eimeo, who sent the letters home to be published. One of these letters, written October 1, 1812, six weeks after his arrival, contained an allusion to Opuhara, whom he seems to have known then as Ariitapoea:

"Dear Friends, War will perhaps soon commence in the district of Papara. We are listening to the reports to find out whether they are true or not. Should war not take place, it will be through fear of us. Enometua is at the head of one party, and Ariitapoea and his brother Tate at the head of the other. Should Enometua be banished from Papara, all Taheite will be involved in war. In this case I shall take Enometua's part, and the Porionuce, which includes all the districts from the isthmus to Tepaerue [Pare Arue?], will join me. Papara and part of Attaharu are for banishing Enometua; but Tacarabei [Ahurai?] and Faa, and part of Attahuru wish to be neuter. We are aware that this war is on our account, and designed to involve us. Perhaps you do not know Enometua, nor Ariitapoea, the brother of Tate who came from Raiatea with Tapoa and party."

This sudden reappearance of Enometua and the old Aromaiterai feud, more than twenty years after it had led to the betrayal of Ariifaa-taia to Pomare (Table VII), rather surprises me, but it led to no harm that I know of. War did not break out. The missionaries returned, and carried on their conversions freely. On the 17th February 1813, Pomare wrote: "Matavai has been delivered up to me. When I am perfectly assured of the sincerity of this surrender, I will write you another letter". The missionaries made a tour of the island; many conversions took place; in Eimeo several idols were publicly burned; there could be no doubt that the Christians were pursuing an active propaganda, and that their success would bring back the authority of Pomare over the whole island; but neither Opuhara nor Tati interfered, and the peace was unbroken.

Yet, after waiting two years at Pare, "vainly expecting the restoration of his government, and endeavoring to recover his authority in his hereditary districts, Pomare returned to Eimeo in the autumn of 1814, accompanied by a large train of adherents and dependents, all professing Christianity". Shortly afterwards, Pomare vahine came up to Eimeo from the Leeward Islands, also with a numerous train of professing Christians. At the same time the Christian converts in Tahiti became an organisation known as the Bure Atua, and everyone could see that Pomare was making use of them, and of his wife's resources, to begin a new effort to recover by force his authority in the island.

War was inevitable, and Pomare with his Christian converts could choose when and where to make it. Pomare himself was not a warrior; he left the active campaigning to his wives, who were less likely to rouse the old enmities. Terite and Pomare vahine came over to Pare Arue in May 1815, with a large party of Christians, and pressed their arrangements for the overthrow of the native chiefs. The chiefs had no choice but to turn them out again, and fixed on the night of July 7 for the combined attack. Opuhara led their forces, and was believed to have given the two queens warning, and to have allowed them time to escape. For his slowness some of the other chiefs charged him with treachery; he replied that he wished no harm to the two women or to their people; that his enemies were the Purionuu; and he marched directly into Pare Arue, and subdued it once more.

While Pomare and the missionaries grew stronger, and, as Ellis expresssed it, became "convinced that the time was not very remote when their faith and principles must rise preeminent above the power and influence" of the native chiefs, the native chiefs themselves showed constant vacillation. In Papara the division became painful. Tati whose connection with Raiatea brought him into close relations with the two Queens, made every effort to prevent war. He could not fail to see that there could be no chance of ever pacifying the islands until they became Christian. With the help of the missionaries and the Raiateans, the Teva chiefs could control Pomare, and the sacrifice of recognising his missionary title of king over the islands, was not so serious, if, at at that price, his ambition could be satiated. If this was Tati's plan, it had the effect of dividing Papara. Opuhara yielded so far as to allow the Christians, within a few weeks, after July 7, to come back to Pare Arue. Pomare himself returned, with all his following, apparently armed and prepared for war. "To maintain the Christian faith, and enjoy a continuance of their present peace and comfort, they foresaw would be impossible ". The native converts were trained to the use of firearms, and the whole missionary interest became for the moment actively militant. The native chiefs, who had no firearms or English allies, and who knew that Pomare meant to subject them once more, still allowed him to return to Pare Arue with a force which had no meaning except for conquest; and to prepare, at his leisure, for the overthrow of their independence.

Under the appearance of religious services Pomare and the missionaries kept their forces under arms. "We had warned our people before they went to Tahiti of the probability of such a stratagem [as an unexpected attack] being practised, should war take place; in conse-quence of which many of them attended worship under arms." With this army numbering "probably about eight hundred" and a war-canoe, with musketeers, besides a second war-canoe "commanded by an Englishman [or Frenchman] called Joe by the natives", and mounting a swivel in the stern, Pomare on November 11, took position at, or near, the village of Punaauia, thirteen-and-a-half kilometres from Pare, and on the edge of Paea and Papara, with pickets far in advance.

This was a challenge which Opuhara, within sight of Punaauia, could hardly decline. He had the best reason to remember Pomare's modes of making war, and there was nothing to prevent Pomare from renewing the surprise and massacre of 1807. Hastily collecting his men, Opuhara rushed towards Punaauia to drive the invaders away. The battle called the Fei-pi -- the ripe plantains -- followed, famous in the missionary annals, and described at length in the missionary histories. From these it appears that Pomare's army, on receiving their scouts' report of Opuhara's advance, which they expected, formed their line on the beach, one flank covered by their war-canoes, the other by a column resting against the hills. Pomare was on the war-canoe that carried the sharp-shooters. The other canoe, with the Englishman Joe from Raiatea, "did considerable execution", and must therefore have taken position to flank and enfilade the attacking party.

Opuhara's attack was violent and broke through the front ranks till it reached the spot where Pomare-vahine and the chief warriors stood. There one of the native missionary converts succeeded in shooting Opuhara, who fell, and shortly afterwards died. His men then broke and retired, unpursued.

This is briefly the story as it is told by Ellis in his "Polynesian Researches" and in the "Missionary Records". Ellis adds:

"Upufara, the last chief of Papara, was an intelligent and interesting man; his death was deeply regretted by Tati, his near relative and successor in the government of the district. His mind had been for a long time wavering, and he was, almost to the morning of the battle, undetermined whether he should renounce the idols, or still continue their votary".

Our traditions tell the story in a different way. According to our old men, Pomare's appearance at Punaauia with his army surprised Opuhara, who had not collected his forces, and would not wait till the men of Taiarapu arrived. He advanced with only half his men, and did not know that the chief of Paea, Temaehuata, had gone over to the Christians without giving him notice of the change. On his advance he met Tati, who had been sent forward to negotiate with him for submission. On coming face to face, Opuhara asked him what he wanted:

"Peace I want with you, my brother!" replied Tati. Opuhara turned away:

"Go, traitor!" he said: "Shame on you! You, whom I knew as my eldest brother, I know no more; and today I call this, my spear, Ourihere, "taeaeneore" "brotherless!" Beware of it, for if it meets you hereafter, it meets you as a foe. I, Opuhara, have stood as Arii on the Moua Temaiti, bowing to no other Gods but those of my fathers. There I shall stand to the end: and never shall I bow to Pomare, or to the Gods forced on us by the white-faced man".

In the ranks of his followers it was firmly believed that Opuhara, few as his forces were, would have won the battle, had not the native missionaries been taught to shoot, as they were taught to pray, and been given guns along with Bibles. The Papara people looked on Opuhara's death as a sort of assassination by a stranger hired and armed for the purpose. They never could understand the white man's system either in war or in peace, and never wholly forgave Tati, although they came to see that Tati was a safer guide than Opuhara. As for submission, they had no longer a choice. When Opuhara fell, their last hope perished. His dying words announced the fall of Papara.

"My children, fight to the last! It is noon, and I, Opuhara, the ti of Moua Temaiti, am broken asunder!"

I am told that Opuhara's spear, "Brotherless Ourihere", is now in the Museum of the Louvre. Even in those days there were among all his warriors only two that could wield it. Among the Tevas he is still regarded as their greatest warrior and hero; and if the missionaries and churches have sometimes doubted whether the natives rightly understood the truths and blessings of

Christianity, perhaps one reason may be that the Tevas remembered how the missionaries fought for Pomare and killed Opuhara.

CHAPTER XVI

From the time of Opuhara's death. Tati became head-chief of the Tevas, and during the next forty years, till his own death, his influence was the strongest in the island. His great task was to keep the peace, and, with all his power and wisdom, his hands were always full. Between the Pomares, the rival districts, the English missionaries and the French fleets, he was seldom without care.

Neither the missionaries nor the natives had any idea of allowing Pomare to fall back into his old ways. They made him refrain from massacre or revenge after the battle of Fei-pi. Although the Papara people could never quite be friends with the man who had murdered their sisters and cousins, Tati succeeded where a weak or a bad man would have only made matters worse. He began by the usual island method of binding Pomare to him by the strongest possible ties. The rapid extinction of chiefly families in Tahiti had left the head-chief of Eimeo or Moorea heir to most of the great names and properties in both islands. Marama, head-chief of Moorea, had only one heir, Marama Arii manihinihi, a woman, and, as I have said, a cousin, or sister in the island mode, of Pomare. This great heiress, almost the last remnant of the three or four sacred families of the two islands, was given by Pomare in marriage to Tati's son, immediately after Tati himself was restored to his rights as head-chief of the Tevas.

Had Pomare possessed a son of his own, he would hardly have let so great a prize go to a rival; and nothing proves so well the new state of discipline to which he had been reduced by Terito, Pomare vahine, the Boraboran and Raiatean chiefs, the missionaries, and Tati himself, as this sacrifice made by a man who was best known for his greed, for the sake of recovering a part of what he had wasted. To secure himself as well as he could from the risk that the Papara family might again turn against him, he did what was usual in such cases; he claimed for his own the first child that Marama should have, and made a compact that the children from the marriage should marry Pomares. When I was born, I was the adopted child of Pomare, and both as Teva, Marama and Pomare, naturally a very great personage. I was not born till after Christianity was established and the Maraes had been abandoned; but my mother, Marama Arii manihinihi, who was born probably about 1800, was carried, after the old island custom, to all her family Maraes at birth -- thirteen of them -- in Moorea and Tahiti. She was Marama at Haapiti, in the island of Moorea; she was Terii vaetua at Faaa; she was Aromaiterai at Papara; she was Teriinui o Tahiti and Maheanuu i Farepua at Vaiari; she was Teriitua Teriiouru maona i Terai i Hitiaa; she was Tetuaraenui ahuri taua o te mauui i Fareroi in Haapape; and with each name she took the lands that belonged to it.

As I have told the story of the Papara family, I will tell that of the Maramas, from tradition, as it is handed down in Moorea. As usual, it begins with genealogy, for we have no history apart from genealogy. The story starts from Punaauia some thirty generations ago. The Punaauia family begins at that point with Nuu, and comes down ten generations to Terii mana, who took a wife from Eimeo, or Moorea, a girl named Piharii of Maraes Nuurua and Farehia. They had two children: a son named Punua teraitua who was chief at Nuurua or Varari, between the two bays on the north shore of the island; and a daughter, Tefeau, who married Tupuoroo, son of Marama, chief of the district of Haapiti on the southwest shore.

Four generations afterwards, the Nuurua chief was named Punua teraitua; the Haapiti chief was named Marama, or properly Terii o Marama i te tauo o te rai, and his Moua was Tahuara, his Outu was Eimeo, his Marae was Marae te fano.

In that generation a small sub-district of Punaauia was occupied by the Atiroos, whose Arii were cousins of Punua teraitua and Marama through Terii mana, four generations back. The degree of relationship never mattered provided the relationship was admitted. The Atiroos had the right to hospitality with their cousins of Nuurua and Haapiti, and some of them came over in six canoes from Punaauia to Nuurua, and were kindly received.

A visit of this sort was a serious matter, for such guests might stay for generations and the full rite of hospitality required that land should be given them to live upon if they chose to remain. The Atiroos did remain with Punua teraitua. But he did not give them land. Their other cousin, Marama, was more generous; he invited them to Haapiti, and set apart the southern and eastern half of his district for them as their residence. They settled there as guests of Marama, and in the course of the next four generations spread over Vaiere, on the east coast, so that they got possession of a number of districts scattered throughout the island.

Then their head-chief felt himself so strong that he declared his independence by setting up a Marae of his own, Te nuu Faatauira, and sending there the sacrifices which had before been sent to Marama's Marae tefano. This was not only as great an insult as they could offer to their host, but it was also a sort of declaration of war, for they took half his territory without tribute or recognition.

The Marama at that time was a woman, Tetupuaiura o terai, and, though neither she nor her people liked to be insulted in this way, she did not care to take up the quarrel with so strong a neighbor. She waited to retaliate, and the Atiroos felt themselves very well able to afford her a chance. They already had half of Haapiti, and they wanted the other half. Their next insult made a blood-feud.

I have already said that kite-flying was one of the favorite native amusements. The young men made huge kites which they raced in rivalry, and the strong southeast trade-wind carried them long distances before they fell. The Atiroos were to have a great feast, with flying of kites, and, in a spirit of mischief, four boys of Marama's people, sons of a woman called Te aropoanaa, planned to take part in the race of kites, though they were not invited. They belonged to the part of the district which the Atiroos had taken, and had suffered under their domineering treatment, until, like boys in other countries, they wanted to pick a quarrel, especially as they knew their superiority at kite-flying. When the feast-day arrived, the Atiroos flew their kites, and while they were watching eagerly to see which flew best, from a neighboring hill four kites started up, more beautiful than theirs, and much faster. These flew over the Atiroos' kites, catching them up and passing them so quickly that the crowd of gazers were struck with awe, not knowing where the strange kites could come from.

The awe quickly gave way to anger. The Atiroos were furious at the insult, and eager to know who had been guilty of it. The elders gave orders to their young men to follow the kites till they fell, to lie in wait for the owners, and to kill them when they appeared. The kites flew high and far; the young men followed them across the mountains into the territory of Taaua itata nuurua, the descendant of Punua teraitua; and at last the kites fell near the Marae of Nuurua. The Atiroos were first on the ground, and when the four boys, following their kites, reached the spot, they were all murdered with the cruelty which was intended in these native feuds to show the utmost expression of contempt, hatred and defiance. The Atiroos had thus committed every possible outrage, including sacrilege.

The boy's mother, Tearopoanaa, waited their return until she knew that they must be in trouble, and then she followed. Of course, such an affair was instantly known to everyone in the neighbourhood. The mother soon found the mutilated bodies of her sons; and probably in presence of crowds of people, with the forms of the most sacred custom, she bathed herself with their blood, and swore revenge.

She was herself not a chief, and could do nothing unless some chief would take up her quarrel. The nearest Arii was the one in whose district, near whose Marae, the sacrilege had been committed, -- Taau-aitatanuurua. To him she went first, and in the due forms claimed his aid. He refused. She then went to Tauraatua, chief of Faatoai, and was refused again. She then went to Tuutini, chief of Mooruu, and was refused a third time. The fourth Arii was Tepau arii umarea chief of Afareaitu, and he too refused.

Moorea or Eimeo is a small island, not quite thirty miles in circuit, and with paths across, at a few points, through mountains which are not so high as those of Tahiti, but more striking in their outlines. The place where the boys were killed, the great central valley of the island, with its two wide and mountain-set bays, has often been called the most beautiful valley in all the South Seas. Remote and solitary now, rarely visited except by professional travellers, like Herman Melville or Captain Cook, it once swarmed with thousands of inhabitants, and was the district against which an army and fleet of ten thousand men were seen by Cook to be collected at Faaa, The chiefs of the island were powerful and numerous. When the Atiroo wars occurred, possibly two hundred and fifty years ago, no chief had any great superiority over the others. Te aro poanaa went to four in succession, and none dared take up her quarrel.

At each place she cut her head with the shark's tooth, and appealed to relationship, telling her story, which was already notorious, yet she got only refusal.

In such a society, where everything was public, the scandal must have been immense; and when Te aro poanaa returned home at night, the whole island must have known that no chief had dared to quarrel with the Atiroos. All the more, everyone must have looked to Marama of Haapiti to see whether she would dare to do what the other chiefs had refused. As soon as Te aro poanaa reached home, her husband asked her whether she had succeeded, and she answered no. He then asked whether she had yet called on Tetupua iura o te rai, -- Marama -- and she said that, absorbed in her grief, she had passed by. Her husband told her to go at once.

She went, and the same scene was acted for the fifth time. She cut her head, told her story, and asked for aid. Marama replied:

"Why have you passed by here, and repassed, and why did you not call for me then ? You have been to the other chiefs before coming here. Still I will take up your cause".

Then Marama called her people to take the woman to the stream of Vaipiura, sacred to Marama and therefore tabu to every one else, and there to wash oif the blood. The drums were beaten at the Marae te-fano and all the people assembled. Marama was seated on the stone seat Pourotonatoofa, "the centre pillar of Notoofa", the Hiva district, and spoke:

"Now the time has come, long waited for. Today has come Te aro poanaa, one of our people, asking revenge for the murder of her sons. I have taken up her quarrel, for I have had the blood washed away in my sacred bath of Vaipiura. Now I call you to be my arms to revenge the death of the four sons of Tearopoanaa, and the insult to my Marae, Maraetefano."

The people rose with the cry: "Your will shall be done. Death to the Atiroos, those in Moorea and those in Tahiti, not one shall live!"

On the hills which divided Marama's people from the Atiroos dwelt two of Marama's warriors -- twins -- Tapuhote and Tetunania, noted for their success in sports. One of them was at the gathering, and returning home arranged with his brother to lead the attack.

They began by cutting in the woods several hundred sticks which they decorated with autis -- leaves of the ti, -- and in the night planted these sticks down the hill bordering the Atiroos' district, to look like warriors. They took down the two main posts of their house, and made them into fighting-spears (omare). This meant that they gave themselves up to the fight, and would never return to their homes.

The Atiroos knew what was coming. Their murder of the boys was a challenge; the mother had gone openly up and down the whole island, bathed in blood, crying for revenge; the drums of Maraetefano had called to arms. By way of further defiance, in the early morning the Atiroos gathered on the shore, at the edge of their district, and while waiting, went into the water, fishing, within Marama's fishing-ground, and, as they killed their fish, called to each other. "Matatuia -- string your fish for the Marae Tenuu Faatauira;" meaning that, for every fish killed, they would kill one of Marama's men for their Marae.

Then the twin Aitos, or warriors, came down the hill, among the sticks which looked like an army of men, and standing out in full view cried: "You make a mistake! String your fish for the Marae of Marae Tefano!" The Atiroo chief called back: "Who dares order sacrifice for Marae Tefano?" "I" called back Tapuhote; "I, with my spear Havivorai! the Sky-swinger! I will swing your head, who call yourself chief of the Atiroos, and I will take you before Marama, and you shall be taken as a sacrifice for Marae Marae Tefano."

With that, throwing his spear, he killed the chief of the Atiroos, and the warriors of Marama, getting among the Atiroos in the confusion that followed their chief's death, led by Tetunania, destroyed them. The bodies of all the chief's family were strung together, and sent to Marama for the Marae of Marae Tefano. The bodies of the common people were also strung together, and sent as an insult to the Marae of Nuurua, for its chief who had first refused to take up the quarrel. The chief of Nuurua sent messengers to say that he would not accept common fish -- pahoros -- as a sacrifice; that at his Marae only the best fish -- uruas -- could be offered. The twins returned word that the Uruas were only for Marae Tefano; and that if pahoros did not satisfy him, he should have a sight of Havivorai. The chief of Nuurua did not venture to take up the challenge, and had to accept the pahoros.

Then the twins gathered their warriors and, crossing the mountains to Opunohu, on the north shore, killed every Atiroo, and took possession of the district for Marama, making of it two new districts called Tupa Ururu and Amehiti.

Then they crossed to Paopao, on the next bay. But some of their warriors had gone ahead of them, and they found on their road the bodies of twins whom the warriors had killed and mutilated. Ashamed to pass them, the Aitos turned off over the mountains to Afare aitu, which they found deserted. One woman named Poivai, a noted beauty came out to meet them, and asked them what they wanted. "We came to kill the Atiroos", they said: "a race we mean to exterminate; but we came not to fight women". So they left Afa-reaitu without taking possession, and went on to Aroa of Vaiere. There they fought and took possession, calling it Teavaro. Thus Mara-ma became master of two thirds of Moorea.

The Atiroos were then all killed or in hiding, and their name was never afterwards heard of in the island: but the twins, collecting their war-canoes, crossed to Tahiti, landing at Faaa, and attacked the Atiroo headquarters in Punaauia, where they were again victorious and went on, across the isthmus of Taravao, to Taiarapu where they killed enough Atiroos to build a Marae with the skulls. And the district is called to this day Teahupoo; that is, Teahu -- a pile, -- and Upoo -- of heads.

This legend of Marama's conquests is singular in being the story of a war which was not for the possession of a woman; but Samson among the Philistines must always have had his Dalilah, and the twin Samsons of Moorea lived among the Philistines of Taiarapu. Yet the variation on the stock legend is curious. The people of Taiarapu, unable to beat the twins in fight, sent a beautiful woman to live with them. They fell in love with her -- both with the same woman, and by her arts were gradually separated from each other, becoming so jealous that they lived apart. She gave them a feast, and got them to drink kava till they were stupified. Then, when she should have called in her people to kill them, she hesitated. As she looked at their magnificent figures at her feet, she found herself in love with them. She kept her oath; perhaps she could not help herself; but when the twins had been put to death, she killed herself with the same spear.

To establish himself in his new territory, Marama came over from Haapiti to Amehiti, and built a Marae there; and there the next Marama, who was a man, was living, when he got his next accession of power. This story is the most Polynesian of all, with no suggestion of myth. The object of the tradition was to explain how Marama, after acquiring nearly all the island except Nuurua and Afareaitu, succeeded in getting those two districts also; and did it in spite of himself.

Two under-chiefs of Afareaitu, called Tuhei and Matafaahira, built a Marae which was to bear the name Horora. They wished to dignify their Marae, and give it the rank of the Maraes of high chiefs, and they selected the chief of Nuuruaas the one whose supremacy they preferred; for, whoever he might be, the chief who mounted their Marae made it and them sacred to himself, -- became in fact the head of their family and the master of their power, much as a feudal lord became master of one who sought vassalage, except that the Tahitian head-chief was both spiritual, temporal and patriarchal head at once; and the chief of Nuurua seemed to be looked upon as the mildest and least aggressive of head-chiefs

Tuhei and Matafaahira went to Nuurua to see the chief, whose official name always remained Punua Teraitua, as it had been when his ancestor received the Atiroos without giving them land, and received Te aro poanaa without taking up her revenge, and received the paho-ros without taking up the challenge of Marama's twin warriors. Teraitua seems to have been the butt of Moorean satire, for the story says that when he heard that Tuhei and Matafaahira were coming, he hid himself that he might not be obliged to see them. The visitors were not to be got rid of in that manner, and as they insisted on seeing him, he had to receive them, which he did at last in the presence of the high-priest Te mooiapitia; but, instead of treating them with respect, he showed complete indifference to their request, declined to give a decided answer, and told them he would consider the matter.

The least civility he could offer was to give them the usual guest-pig, and the pig was ordered to be killed and cooked, but while the feast was preparing, the messengers arrived who had been sent by Tuhei and Matafaahira in advance, and had tarried on the road. To the astonishment of Temoo, the high priest, the messengers were received with more courtesy than had been shown to their masters, and to his still greater astonishment, at the feast the best part of the pig was given to the messengers while the intestines were passed to the masters. Temoo then said to the two under-chiefs: "You see how Teraitua has ridiculed your request and has shown his contempt by giving you the intestines of the pig. What more do you want? Return home, and mount your Marae of Horora yourselves". They said: "No! our people wait; all is ready; and our minds are made up, and declared to the people, that our Marae of Horora shall be mounted by one higher than ourselves". "Then why not ask Marama?" said the high-priest; "He will receive you with more courtesy and treat you with less contempt."

So Tuhei and Matafaahira went on from Nuurua to Amehiti, and arrived there after Marama had gone to sleep under the effects of his kava. The natives still show the cave where Marama drank kava and where no sound was permitted; not even the crowing of a cock, that his repose should not be disturbed. The chief's person was sacred when under the influence of kava, and the man who dared to disturb him did so at the risk of his life. The two under-chiefs, who were in haste to get their ceremony at the Marae performed, could not wait, and went to the priest for advice. He told them to take the sleeping Marama on their backs, and risk the consequences of carrying him off. They followed the advice, and each taking one of Marama's legs, were carrying him off, when Marama awoke and asked who they were and what they wanted.

"We are Tuhei and Matafaahira", they answered.

"Welcome, then, to Amehiti", said Marama.

"We need welcome, for we come to beg a favor. Come with us to Afareaitu, and mount our Marae of Horora."

"Your request must wait till I can call my districts. Atituhaui and Fanauaraa; Atitanei and Tefanaautaitahi; Rotu and Tefarerii; Porotona-toofa, Amehiti and Tupaururu. Marama cannot go alone without his two Vaa (canoes; i.e. districts.)"

"We will be your Vaa", they replied: "We pray you to be satisfied with Amehiti and Tupaururu who are at hand."

Marama at last consented, and was carried over the mountains to Afareaitu, where he mounted the Marae of Horora. The third chief of Afareaitu, Tepauarii, who had not taken part in the proceeding, heard the drums, and asked what they meant. When he was told, he said: "Be it so! Marama is worthy, and I too bow my head to him."

Thus Marama was chosen chief of Afareaitu, and became head of that district as well as of those he had inherited and those he had conquered. In the meanwhile Terai tua of Nuurua becoming conscious of his mistake, had called his people to carry him to Afareaitu, but on the way learned that his place had been taken, and he too bowed his head to the choice.

The last step in Marama's supremacy was the marriage of his son to Terai tua's daughter, which brought Nuurua into the family, and gave the Maramas nearly the whole island.

CHAPTER XVII

Every great name had a sort of legend or title attached to it, to make known in formal oratory or poetry the eminence of the chief. The verses which told the dignity of Marama were these:

Terii o Marama i te tauo o te rai.

Lord Moon of the summit of the sky.

Eimeo and Nuurua bow down to you.

You surpass the heads of Taaroa and Tane.

You are the lord circled by the rainbow,

As you stand on Punaauia

You are the child of Raamaurire

Who was a lord and still a God.

You wear the golden Maro of Maraetefano.

As the land grew, You grew as lord of Eimeo.

Whatever might be meant in Tahiti by the word Arii rahi or Terii, and whether or no the idea of kingship ever existed there, as a complete one for the whole island, there is no kind of doubt that in the island of Moorea and in the case of Marama the idea of supremacy was as complete and exclusive as ever it was with Charlemagne. The districts under him were commanded by fighting chiefs, like Maheine whom Cook knew in 1777 as chief of Opunohu, and Hamau whom he knew as chief of Maatea, and Terii tapunui, chief of Vaiere; but neither Cook nor any of the other foreigners seems to have come in contact with Marama.

I have already said that the Marama of Cook's time, and the elder Otoo of Cook's acquaintance, married first cousins. The Terii vaetuas of Tefana i Ahurai made the bond that united or divided the three powers between which the district of Tefana stands. Purea, Teihotu and Auri, the three children of Terii vaetua, were the three channels along which the story has run (Table IV). Purea's quarrel with her own family caused the overthrow of Papara and the elevation of Pare Arue. Pomare-Vairatoa, born about 1743, married Teihotu's daughter; Marama, in the same generation, married Auri's daughter, both of them Purea's nieces, and all three of the Ahurai family. When the second Pomare, in 1808, was at last driven out of Tahiti, he took refuge in Moorea with his cousin, and even after he had been brought back in 1815, and was undisputed King of Tahiti, he always treated Marama as a social superior.

Tati yielded the same position to her, after she married his son. When I was born, about 1824, I naturally became a petted child, and sometimes treated my mother with as little respect as petted children are apt to show. Old Tati would then scold his granddaughter, and would tell me that no one had ever, even in fun, dared to speak to Marama in any tone but one of deep respect. Nevertheless Tati's whole authority as chief of Papara and head-chief of the Tevas could not prevent the atmosphere of Papara from being saturated with hostility to everything related to Purionuus and Pomares, or oblige the people to recognise all that he had conceded for himself. Indeed his daughter-in-law Marama could not even get possession of the lands she owned in Papara as Arornaiterai, and she did not venture to insist on their being given up to her. As one daughter after another came into the world, she grew more and more interested to secure their inheritance, but she did not know what lands belonged to Aromaiterai, and neither Tati nor anyone else would tell her. Not daring to fret her father-in-law further, she waited till I became old enough to understand what she wanted, and set me to the task. Every morning I was obliged to take my place by Tati's side, and pet him into good-humor. In those days the family lived in native fashion, in one large house, sleeping on the mats, under tapa sheets, the children with their parents; and in the early morning the children ran about as they pleased. Tati was then an elderly man, past fifty, big and rough in appearance to a young child, though kind and affectionate, as natives almost always are. He suspected that his grand-daughter had some motive in her attentions, and teased her to tell him, but she was afraid. The secret came out at last, and she won from the old man what her mother had not been able to win for herself; but she never forgot how little she liked the duty.

Papara was never my mother's favorite residence, and Papeete still less so. At that time Papeete had hardly grown to be even the European town it has since become. Papara was at least native, even though it was clannish and jealous of power; but Papeete was not even a chief's residence, for the Otoo or Pomare family lived on the point of Outuaiai, three or four miles from Papeete to the eastward, in Arue, and their Marae of Tarahoe was also in Arue. No native tradition or dignity was associated with Papeete, which grew into consequence only on account of its harbour; and, as a resort of foreign ships and seamen, was never held in favor by respectable chiefs, whose current of life flowed in native channels, as far from foreign Papeete as possible. Marama always preferred her own island to Tahiti, and there she lived by preference. In almost every portion of Moorea she was at home. In Haapiti, starting-point of the Maramas, she bore the name of Tupua i ura o te rai. In Maatea she was Teriimana i Ahurai; in Afareaitu she was Tepau arii i Umarea; in Teavaro she was Marama; in Moruu she was Aromaiterai; in Vaiere she was Tutapu; in Varari she was Narii i te rauaru. In all these places she was mistress in her own right and over Haapiti as a whole she was chiefess in her own right, and a much more important person than her husband, who was overshadowed by Tati's great authority. I think the women of our family have inherited this preference for the Moorea, and have felt themselves more at home there than elsewhere.

I was the eldest child of Tapua taaroa and Marama, born probably in 1824, at Vaiari. From my father I received the name Teriirere i Tooarai; from my mother the name of Ariioehau; and as I had been claimed by Pomare, I received from his side the name Taaroa, although he was dead before I was born. In old days the eldest child of a head-chief was always carried at its birth to the family Maraes as sacred, with offerings to the Gods. In the island society any person who could say that one of his parents had been carried to the Marae asserted his high birth; any one who could say that both parents had been carried stood at the head of society; but anyone who could say that all four of her parents, by birth and adoption, had been carried, enjoyed a rare social distinction, and therefore even the Pomares, far from showing jealousy, regarded and treated me as one of themselves.

Marama had little to do with her daughter. Mothers were not much consulted in regard to their eldest child, or indeed in regard to any child, if the family claimed it. Children in this communistic society were as much the objects of exchange or gift, as any other article of property, and were begged quite as commonly. Although I was born at Vaiari, the Papara people at once claimed me, and built for me a special house, the fareoa, usually built for the children of Arii, and sacred even to the parents. They placed it on a small point where two branches of a stream join to empty into the sea, a stone's throw from Tati's house. The fareoa was peculiar in having but one roof-post, and in being sacred. The attendants were also sacred; the child was fed by servants who were sacred, and who had charge of her to the exclusion of the mother.

This arrangement was broken up by Terito, Pomare's widow, who carried out the idea of her husband by claiming me, and by coming to Papara to take me away; which she actually did, and carried me to Papaoa, the Pomares' residence in Arue. Terito's own daughter Aimata was ten or twelve years older than I, born probably in 1812 or 1813, but the two girls were brought up together, under the care of Uata, a man who for a number of years exercised the powers of government, such as they were; and always had the respect and confidence of natives and foreigners. The story of these times is written in a number of heavy books which any one can read, and which have lost the interest they had fifty years ago, when France and England were quarrelling over poor little Tahiti. I am not going to tell the tale over again. I am not even going to tell what Tati did, in the forty years during which he was struggling to prevent the islands from falling back into chronic wars and disturbances. I am concerned only with what is not printed, and what has a connection with our family.

Uata was an interesting man. He was a friend of the second Pomare, and was made feeding-father or guardian of the boy, the third Pomare, who was born in 1820. Pomare II died December 7, 1821, leaving the daughter Aimata, a girl not yet nine years old, and the boy, Pomare III, a child in arms. Aimata was never regarded with favor by Pomare, her father, who was very frank in saying that she was not his child; so the boy was made king. Moerenhout says that Pomare, on his death-bed, wished Tati to take the government, but that the missionaries and other chiefs were afraid to trust Tati, and preferred to take the charge of the boy on themselves. This is likely enough, although I doubt whether Tati asked such a responsibility, and those that knew Tati best would suspect that he was greatly relieved at escaping it.

So Uata became in effect the head of the Pomare family and the chief adviser in all difficult questions. The missionaries in due time went through the formal ceremony of crowning the infant, April 22, 1824, at Papaoa, and then took him to their school, the South Sea Academy which was established in March, 1824, in the island of Moorea at Papetoai. There he was taught to write, and educated in English which became his language, until he was seven years old, when he fell ill, and was taken over to his mother at Pare, where he died, Jan. 11, 1827. In his last illness he called constantly for water, using the English word, for he had never learned the native language. His feeding-father, who did not understand English, brought him every sort of food he could think of, but still the child cried for water. This is said to have been the cause of the name Uata, which his feeding father took after his death, on becoming the guardian of Aimata, as the queen, Pomare IV, was always called by natives.

Aimata when a girl of about nine years, in December, 1822, was married or betrothed to Tapoa of Huahine and Borabora. As I grew up, I became her most intimate friend, and Uata was our constant adviser. The unfortunate Aimata had troubles of every sort, domestic, political, private and public, until at last the missionaries, English and French, fought so violently for control of her and the island that she was fairly driven away. Among other laws which the English missionaries were supposed to have obtained to prevent strangers from obtaining influence in the island, was one of March 1,1835, forbidding strangers under any pretext, from marrying in Tahiti or Moorea. I did not choose to marry any native then to be found in the island. Terito, the queen mother, tried to get up a match between me and one of the Raiatea chiefs, but my mother, Marama, did not think the marriage good enough. Finally I decided to marry Mr Salmon, an Englishman who had general esteem and consideration in the island; and Aimata suspended the law in order to enable her friend to be married.

CHAPTER XVIII

Tahiti ran along curiously like Europe in her seasons of war and peace. The coincidence which made her a sort of shambles during the time of the long European wars, led to the coincidence that the year 1815 should have been the close of her age of violence, although I know no special reason why she should have been affected by the battle of Waterloo, or the European peace, or why the missionaries should have succeeded just then, without apparent effort, in obtaining the military strength which they had failed to get when Pomare was more powerful. At all events, for forty years or thereabouts, the missionaries ruled the islands; and, considering that the islands contained only five thousand inhabitants, or a few more or less, the missionaries and the islands made an immense noise in the world, and left a library of literature strewn along their track. Pomare became a name almost as well known in Europe as that of Louis Philippe. I am not going to tell the story of the missionary rule, or of the share which Tati took, during those years, in the island politics, for it can be read in dozens of books, from Moerenhout downwards, and the story, besides being dull, is one which still stirs up temper. The missionary reign was long, and, as far as I know, Tati and the Tevas gave it no trouble; but the day came at last when the sway of the missionaries was broken, and Tati had to suit himself to new conditions. He was still chief of Papara, but an old man, when the trouble came, and his grand daughter was the most intimate friend of Aimata, the Queen. Of course, the new dangers were common to them all.

Fifty years ago, everyone in the civilised world knew that, in 1836, two French missionaries landed at Tahiti to convert, not pagans but Protestant Christians, to the faith of Rome. The missionaries who ruled Tahiti, indignant at this interference, invoked the aid of the British Consul Pritchard, who caused the Queen to order their arrest and expulsion. The order was executed Dec. 12, 1836.

The two French missionaries made a protest to their government, and King Louis Philippe sent a frigate to Papeete with the usual message of great powers to little ones,-- an ultimatum, to which the Queen naturally acceded, as small powers always have done, and always must do, before great ones.

Then began a struggle on the part of Consul Pritchard and the London missionaries to recover their ground, which led to a letter from Queen Pomare to Queen Victoria suggesting a British protectorate, whereupon the French government sent another frigate to Tahiti, in 1839, and made Aimata repeat her submission.

As the British government had at that time very little sentiment about missionaries, and Sir Robert Peel had a very precise knowledge of the value of unclaimed islands all over the world, Queen Victoria did not accept the advance made by Pomare, and the missionaries were again thrown on their own resources. Then the chiefs broke loose from the missionaries, and in September, 1841, decided that, between such masters as England and France, they could not hope to maintain independence or even a good understanding; and since England would not undertake to protect them, they Would try to obtain protection from France. So they drew up the necessary papers for the Queen to approve; but a British frigate arrived at that moment, and this reinforcement of the British interest decided Aimata to refuse to sign.

The next August another French squadron arrived, and the chiefs again took counsel, with the admiral's aid and advice. They arrived at the same decision they had reached the previous year; and it is hard to see how they could reach any other. The letter which they wrote, Sept. 9, 1842, to the admiral Du Petit-Thouars, gave the conclusive reasons for the step, and is proof enough of their intelligence.

"Inasmuch as we cannot continue to govern ourselves so as to live on good terms with foreign governments, and we are in danger of losing our island, our kingdom, and our liberty, we, the Queen and the high chiefs of Tahiti write to ask the king of the French to take us under his protection."

This paper was signed by four chiefs, of whom Tati was one. It was then sent to Aimata at Eimeo, and, after much hesitation, she also signed. The French Admiral, on September 30, 1842, hoisted the flag of the protectorate; and the chiefs, no doubt, were happy to think that at last their anxieties were partially thrown on stronger shoulders.

Far from it! Pritchard returned from England, Feb. 25, 1843, and declared violent war against the French. Queen Pomare obeyed his wishes, and refused to obey those of the Freneh Admiral. Du Petit-Thouars, on thgse considerations, lost his temper; landed troops; took possession of the island; declared the Queen deposed; and, when disturbances began, which he believed to be fomented by Pritchard, he arrested Pritchard and turned him roughly out of the island.

The English and French press, on this news, made an outcry that deafened Europe; but Louis Philippe disavowed the Admiral, and ordered him to return to the Protectorate. Unfortunately the shock of these violent changes had already disturbed the peace at Tahiti; Aimata fled to a British ship and then to Raiatea; her people at Mahaena and Hitiaa -- the whole Pomare connection -- took up arms, and established themselves close to Papeete; in short, another civil war broke out. In this case, however, the quarrel was between the Pomares and the Europeans who had hitherto been their allies. Tati took no share in the revolt, but not a few of the Tevas joined it, and the years of 1844 and 1845 were a season of fighting and marching, sometimes severe and always exhausting to the combatants on both sides.

At this point, in February, 1846, begins my own story of how I interposed, as chiefess, to bring about peace, and the submission of the islanders to French rule. I repeat it in my own words which are more lifelike than any that an editor could use.

THE STORY OF ARIITAIMAI, 1846.

During the year 1846 I was resting myself in my room at our house in Papeete, when an old woman by the name of Peutari was shown in. At her entrance I could see that she was very much grieved about something, and a little while after she entered the room she cried out: "I cry for my land of Tahiti. Our people will soon be at war with the French, and they will soon be opened like a lot of chickens?" These words startled me and gave me great pain. She repeated these former words and added: "Don't you know that you are the first of the island, and it remains in your hands to save all this and your land?" Other words followed from this woman, which led me to make up my mind to go and see the French governor, Bruat. I prepared myself then to visit this governor. When he saw me walking up the alley way towards the government house, he came out to meet me, and said: "What brings you here so early?" I then asked an audience with him in his room, and sent for an interpreter, so that he would fully understand what I wished. I then made known to him what I had decided to do, saying that I had heard it spoken of in the town that the frigate Uranie and her tender, the steamer Phaeton, were both going to be sent around to Papeenoo full of troops to fight the natives. Bruat replied, saying; "You have heard the truth. The Colonel commanding the troops of the town has heard of so many instances of insult given to the French that we have decided, at last, to go out and finish up the affair." I then requested the governor to allow me some time to go out and see if I could not make peace with these people. Before authorizing these steps, however, he sent for the commander of the troops, who informed us after his arrival, that orders had gone out to the outpost at Point Venus to prevent any people passing to the native armies beyond, and that in order for me to pass, it would be necessary that an officer should be sent with us. He then asked me by whom I was to be accompanied and my object in going. I told him that my relation, Ariipaea, had agreed to go with me. We then prepared for our journey. He told me that he would send his own aide-de-camp with us. I left him, he wishing me all success. On my arrival at the house, I found the old woman Peutari still there, and when I informed her that the governor had promised to aid in preventing this bloodshed, she began to weep.

I was no sooner ready than a note arrived from the governor, sending me his own and his wife's horses as a means of transport. We then started upon our journey, arriving at the first outpost Taharaa. We found the troops there under arms and preparing to enforce the orders. Letters, however, delivered to the commander of these troops stopped their advance, and there the governor's aide-de-camp returned to town. Our passports were given here, and myself with my relation continued on our trip alone. Arriving at Point Venus, we were made to show our passports, and then were allowed to continue to our destination. Both of us were very much afraid, on seeing all of these men drawn up with their arms, ready for the march; but we plucked up our courage, and thoroughly intended to see the end of our object. My relation Ariipaea, however, was more afraid of our own natives than of the French, as lately he had deserted his own side. I, however, knew my influence with the natives would be sufficient to save him from any trouble whatever. We very soon arrived at the third outpost of the

French at Tafai. We passed through this outpost without difficulty. We rested a while when there, as we saw there some of our old friends who had sided with the French, who kept us for breakfast. We were lucky to have accepted this invitation to stay to breakfast, as we were told then that a man named Aifeuna, with his companion, Nohoraa, had inquired what was the object of our visit, and when they were told we were on our way to Papenoo to offer peace to the natives, they had said they would never allow Ariipaea to pass with his life. They were seen to have gone on to the point of a hill a little beyond, with their muskets, with the full intention of shooting him and perhaps myself; these two men having suffered from the natives.

These two intended murders, however, were prevented by the people with whom we had taken our meal. We then rode on. Arriving at a point beyond, we saw a small detachment of the native troops, consisting of ten or twelve men, who were burning a small house on the beach. When they saw us riding up, they called out to stop, or they would fire on us. I recognized the first, a young man in this small detachment, and when he recognized me, he ran up and cried out, "What news do you bring?" I simply said that I wanted to see the chiefs in command, and asked him where they were. He said: "They are in the fort." I inquired which one of the forts, and he replied: "The one at Poroporo." I asked again where was Ori. Ori was a half brother of my father's. He replied: "He is in Papenoo." We continued riding as fast as we could, and everywhere on our route we saw people running about in great excitement, as the news of the two steamers coming to bombard the village had already arrived before us, and they were making their way into the bush, with all they could of their utensils. Arriving at the nearest part of the fort, I called out to a young man that I had previously known, who ran out to us and took our horses, and led us on foot up to the fort. This man, however, I sent ahead, to inform the chiefs, that I knew well, to come out of the fort and meet me. About half way up to the fort, three of these chiefs came out, and cried with pleasure when they saw me. One of the three was Pihato, a son of the old chief of Papenoo, who was the head man in the fort. Arato was another. He was a brother in law of Ori, my uncle. I then asked these three men where all of the chiefs were collected, and they said that they were then in their different forts. I then told the head man to try, if possible, to collect all these chiefs in one place, with as many men as possible, as I had something very serious to put before them. He then decided to have our meeting take place in the village of Papenoo itself, and at once led me to the town hall of this village.

At the entrance to the village, Teavaava and the people of Hitiaa and Tiarai, with their chiefs, Manua and Teriitua, with the principal men of their districts, were all in their fort. Near this fort was a large house into which we entered. In this house I found a brother of the chief, Manua, the chief Aru; Taute, Aiani, and Kama -- all men holding chief's commands. Those from Hitiaa, I knew. There I saw Teriitua, herself, and Teohu and Tumoehamia. These two were in command of that district. Teriitua, who was my aunt, caught me by my legs and began to cry. One of the chiefs then brought me a stool. My aunt then asked me why I was there. Knowing that this person, with her two men in command, held the power of Teono, and wishing to explain to them the object of my visit before the arrival of the rest, I at once told them what I intended to do, and asked her to help me in carrying out my object, as I was afraid that without gaining her on my side, those of the Teporionuu would do their best to go against my peaceful intention. In a little while the chiefs began to arrive at this meeting, and I saw the chief men who represented the Pomares, Teaa-toro and Nuutere. I, however, saw the latter Nuutere, coming, and I walked out of the house to meet him. As soon as he saw me he came towards me, and even before saluting me, said: "What have you to do here?" I continued walking, and took him by the hand, and said to him: "My object in coming here is to bring peace, and I have counted upon you for the sake of old friendship to be my speaker in this trying instance." I could see that he was very much perplexed in this, for I had heard that he would probably be the first one to refuse the offer of peace. Being, however, alone, for he had not seen Ariipaea, he could not leave me, a lone woman, to speak out before all these men, and therefore he assented to my request. The people then were continuing to arrive, and in very little while, most of the head chiefs were there together. The house being unable to hold every one, our meeting was proposed to be taken to the church building. Teohu then came forward and said to me: "Let us all go!" I called Nuutere to be near me. I then explained to him what I intended him to ask in my name. I informed him that I had seen the French governor, who had given me only a short time to come and meet with these people in their different camps, to present to them a proposition of my own to undertake to prevent bloodshed. He then called first Teaatoro. They talked together a little while without my hearing them, and just before entering the church, Nuutere whispered to me that Teaatoro would be all right. I could see that pretty near the whole of the island was represented at this meeting, those of Tautira only being absent.

After they had heard the object of my visit amongst them, Teaatoro got up as the chief speaker, and stated in the name Tu: "We are all as one person in this meeting, and we have suffered together as brothers. We have heard what the object of this lone woman's visit amongst us is -- solely for our good and that of our children. What can we say to this? We can only return her one answer, which is to thank her for the trouble and danger she has taken upon herself for the peace she has brought, and she must return to the French commander with this, our answer. We have been here for months, on the point of starvation. We have lost a great many of our men by fighting. We lost a great many at Taravao. The best of our blood was spilled at Mahaena. At Piha-e-atata, our young men were slain. Our queen left us in the midst of our troubles and went away to a different island without the least sorrow for us. We have heard no words of the help which was promised us by Great Britain." Another of the chiefs then got up, named Roura. This one turned to me and said: "Ariitaimai, you have flown amongst us, as it were, like the two birds Rua taa and Teena. Your object was to join together Urarii and Manu, and you have brought them into this valley. You have brought the cooling medicines of vainu and mahainui-eumu into the hearts of the chiefs that are collected here. Our hearts yearn for you, and we cannot in words thank you; but the land, one and all, will prove to you in the future that your visit will always remain in their memory. You have come personally. I have heard you speak the words out of your own mouth. You have brought us the best of all goods, which is peace. You have done this when you thought we were in great trouble, and ran the risk of losing our lives and property. You have come forward as a peace-maker for us all."

The other chief repeated pretty nearly the same words. Those, however, who represented amongst this group my own district, said: "As you are my head, my eyes, my hands and my feet, what more can I say? what you have decided, we accept and will carry out."

One man amongst them then got up, a man named Haururu, and turning around to the other chiefs, called out, in a very loud voice, and said: "Why have you decided upon this peace so soon? Tahiti is not broken asunder. We could play with the French until we could get aid of Great Britain, who has formally promised to help us through in this war. I think you have all done wrong, and if Great Britain hears of this new state of affairs, she will altogether withdraw her help from us."

My speaker replied to him and said: "Where were you, that consider yourself such a fighting man, in the fights that have already happened? I have never perceived you ahead of the others. You do not excel the youngest of our men in all of these battles. What have you got to say? What are you known as in the annals of the country, which allows you to get up and speak when your chiefs have already given the word? If peace had not been declared here amongst us all, your blood would have to pay for this insult."

The meeting then broke up. It was then about two o'clock in the afternoon, and as I had to arrive in Papeete before midnight, the time allowed me by the governor as a limit to which he would wait in giving out new orders for taking these forts, I had to make all haste to prepare for the journey. We had hardly finished when the Teva, represented by two of their chiefs, arrived. These, however, being one of ourselves, I was confident what they would say. As they were arriving at the house, I went forward myself and spoke to them in person, telling them not to feel hurt that the meeting had gone on without them; that I had given my word for them to the others. Moearu replied at once: "Our chiefess, you have done right." They stayed then on the outside, and did not enter the house. We then went to Ori's house to rest ourselves for a little while. Most of the head-men followed me, and offered to aid us on our way. Whilst we were there, the man Haururu then tried to create trouble amongst the young men of the different districts collected there, proposing to stop the peace that had already been decided upon by their chiefs, and to continue on, by stealth, and come to and beat out the first outpost of the French. The news of this new trouble was brought to me by some of our own men of Taiarapu, who told me of what had been done during my absence and the absence of the chiefs from the meeting house. This new state of affairs decided me to write to my husband in

Papeete to ask him to see the governor, and tell him that the object of my visit had been decided upon, and to request him, at the same time, for a truce of twelve more hours, telling the messenger not to mention anything whatever about the last trouble, and that I would, myself, leave early in the morning to return to Papeete.

I then went to the house of my aunt, Teriitua, where I intended to sleep, for I was very tired after this hard day's work. I could not, however, take my rest until very late, because news began coming in all the time, which troubled me, and I was afraid that the ringleaders would increase and undo what had already been done. Teohu and Ori, however, assured me that I need not trouble myself any more about it; that the head chiefs had decided what was to be done, and that was final; that if these ringleaders continued to make trouble they would be shot.

Later on, four of the chiefs arrived. They came and asked me what would happen to the queen Pomare, in this peace, and whether I would go and bring her from Raiatea, where she had taken refuge. I said to them that so far as peace was concerned, I did not think it would do any harm to the queen, and that I would certainly be willing to continue to act as a peacemaker and would go to Raiatea and bring her back to her own country. They then requested me to do so, and to try all that I could with her to get her to come back to her own home. They said: "When you arrive on that island, tell her from us that she must write to us and inform us the object of the visit of the English admiral in Raiatea, and whether England, or Great Britain, has withdrawn her promise of help given us heretofore; and that she must write to us and inform us whether yes or no, and whether we are to accept the French government altogether."

Early in the morning I and my friend started on our return. Ten of the chiefs escorted us. On arriving at the first outpost of the French, we saw a troop of men having two natives amongst them, one of them a man named Paete, who was a judge in the district of Papeete. They were preparing to leave, with the intention of attacking one of the principal forts. Our escort left us there, and as soon as the French heard that there was a truce still continuing, orders were given for the men to return to their positions.

I made all the haste possible to arrive in the town of Papeete before the expiration of the time I had asked for, in which I succeded. did not even call at my own home, but went straight up to the governor's house. The governor, having seen me at a distance, riding up, came outside to meet me and help me off my horse. He understood a little Tahitian, and said: "Is it peace?" I replied that it was peace, and that everything was all right. He held my hand, and said: "The Tahitians should never forget you; but do not consider your work finished. You must now prepare to leave and to go to Raiatea." I told the governor that I would follow out his instructions, and I would certainly go; but that I had to consult my grandfather, Tati. When the old man heard that I was preparing to leave for Raiatea, he came, and with a troubled face, said to me: "Are you really going to fetch the queen, and bring her back to this country?" I told him that I was going to do so. This affected him a great deal, but he did not say why. In leaving, however, he simply said these words: "Do your duty!" We at once made preparations to go on this trip. My husband and Arii-paea were to accompany me. The governor had ordered the steamer Phaeton to be prepared, and we were to leave at twelve o'clock that day for Huahine. Orders were given on board the steamer to the commander of the vessel that he was to follow my orders in everything concerning where the vessel should go. On the next day we arrived at Huahine, where I was very well received by my old relations. We stayed there a few hours, and continued on our route for Raiatea, where we safely arrived. A boat was at once sent with a message, and our letters, to the queen. These were sent by Ariipaea, who, however, was obliged to return, as he was fired upon. In a little while, however, a man named Moemoe seemed to have recognized us from one of the islands, and pulled off in a canoe. He became then the bearer of our letters. In a short time we received a reply from the queen Pomare, who wrote me to say that Tamatoa, her uncle, and Tehaapapa, her aunt, would not allow her to receive us on shore, as we belonged to the French side, but that if we would go on to an island and let the vessel go back to Huahine at once, we might then come ashore. This we would not hear of, as we were afraid that as soon as the French vessel left we should all be murdered. We, however, continued at our anchorage during that night. Early in the morning, an old nurse of ours named Ino, and a relation of ours, Tahitoe, came on board and met me. In a little while there came off a boat from the shore, sent by the queen to bring us there. They had changed their minds at a meeting held the evening before. We were then taken to Vairahi, where we found the queen Pomare, with all of her relations about her. She cried very much when she saw me, and very soon the whole place was filled. Tamatoa and Terii maevarua were also present.

Ariipaea spoke for us, and told the queen that the object of our visit was to take her back to her island, and submit to the French; that we were authorized by the governor of the French to tell her that all of the past and her own action in breaking up the agreement which was entered into with the French would be overlooked for this time, and that they would continue to honor her and accept her as queen of Tahiti.

Her spokesman, her uncle, replied, saying: "What you have spoken is good for the queen of Tahiti. We know that she is queen of Tahiti, and she has therefore everything to say to her people; but you forget that Pomare is our guest. She gave herself up into our hands, and we have made our minds up that we will protect her, and no harm shall ever come to her during her stay with us."

My husband then spoke and told these people of the harm that they were doing the queen whom they pretended to love, and that if they did not accept the conditions which the French had offered, she would altogether lose her own power on the island.

These arguments seemed to trouble them, for Tapoa, a powerful chief at once replied: "You are right, and these are wrong. We have not the power to go to Tahiti and force the French away from that island, and put this queen in their place." Pomare seemed to me very weak-minded at that meeting, for she did not say a word. She kept crying on. My husband then spoke to her, and said: "What have you got to say? Can't you say something for yourself and for your own government, or have you forgotten that you are the queen of Tahiti, and that these people here have nothing in common with you?"

The speaker replied at once, and said: "We are trusting to the help of Great Britain, who has promised us to send ships and men to fight our cause, and to keep us an independent state."

The queen herself then said: "I trust to the word of Great Britain, and I will not return and be under the French." My husband then replied by saying: "Now we have your own words, and I beg of you to reconsider them. If you do not wish to go back, give us your eldest son or your mother, and let us go to Tahiti and accept the protectorate for them." Tamatoa got up in a rage and said: "We will not permit any of the Pomare sons or anything belonging to her to return to Tahiti." Ariipaea then got up and said: "We have now heard your reply to the French governor of Tahiti, and we wish now to inform you of the word sent through us by the chiefs of Tahiti; they wish to be informed through you of the engagement you have taken with Great Britain, which was arranged here between you and the admiral. You must inform them of it, and we have given our word to be the bearer of your letter to them, in reply to their demand."

We could see then that this seemed to trouble them a great deal and they appeared to be undecided what to do, or what answer to give to the demands of the chiefs of Tahiti. Queen Pomare then asked me aside: "Have you been to the wars or to the forts?" I replied: "Yes!"; that I had been there, and how sorry I felt at seeing them in the state they were, poor, with hardly clothes enough to wear, and very near to the point of starvation, and I said: "You must write to them, somehow or other."

This seemed to trouble her a great deal, but she said nothing. On that day we saw the frigate Uranie going from Huahine, and we were told that Mai and Tefaaora, men of Borabora, were aboard of her. This frigate, I was told by the governor in Tahiti, was to go and anchor in the harbor at Huahine, awaiting the results of our visit to Raiatea. These two men having decided for the French, were obliged to leave their island to save their lives. The French had sent this frigate down there, thinking that these islands were also under the government of Pomare.

We then returned to Tahiti. After a few days governor Bruat sent again for me, and said that I had better go back to Raiatea, and continue what I had already done. We prepared a second time to go, and this time we went by a small cutter boat. At that time I took over with me my little daughter. We had a dreadful trip going over in this small cutter, and on my arrival at Vaiarahi, I found that the chiefs who had met there before were absent, as my visit was unknown to any of them. I therefore found Queen Pomare alone, and I stayed with her quite a long time. My husband was sent to Huahine, to arrange to make peace with that island, and the French frigate Uranie. The French were then trying to arrange for the independency of these little islands, as they did not belong to the government of Pomare at all. Tahiti and Moorea and the lower archipelago were the only ones that were under the government of the Pomares. My husband then came back to Raiatea to us and told the queen that as soon as the peace was arranged the Uranie would leave for Tahiti; but she was however obliged to make two trips before that was settled. He then returned to inform the queen of the result and success of his arrangements, before leaving for Tahiti. At the same time he asked her again to come back to her own land, and put herself under the French protectorate that she had already signed documents for. She then replied to us, unexpectedly, that she would do so, but for us not to be in too much of a hurry. The governor's representative on board of the vessel then returned to Tahiti.

My husband then returned to Tahiti with Ariipaea, and during our absence the battle of Punaauia had already been fought. He and Ariipaea were then sent off to Punaauia, and succeeded in making peace, after which they came to Raiatea, to join me, and to again ask the queen to go to her government. Whilst we were still there, the news arrived fhat another of the battles of Punaauia had taken place, and the French commander Brea had been killed, and the second in command wounded [30 May, 1846]; that the French had been badly beaten in that valley. On account of this victory of the natives, the queen seemed to have changed her mind again, for she imagined that the Tahitians would at last make head against the French, and drive them out of the country. I had then been two months in Raiatea with her, trying with all my power to get her to come home. The chiefs, during my absence, had again reunited, and decided that they would not enter into an agreement with the French as long as the queen was away, and that she had to come there first and make her submission, before they would do so. There were people on the island giving her advice contrary to ours, and they seemed to be gaining more ground with her, which hurt me very much, as our own affairs on the island were going badly on account of our absence, and the whites of Tahiti were simply using my name as traitress to her country.

The queen, however, promised, at last, that she would leave by a small schooner called Ana. I then waited for the arrival of that schooner, and when she arrived, I saw the captain and made arrangements for him to take us all to Tahiti. He told me that the vessel was at my command, and that I could do what I liked with it, and that I had only to name the day for leaving, when she would do so. The first week passed without anything being decided, although every day I told the queen that we must leave. When it came to the end of the second week, my patience began to be exhausted, I then spoke again to her to get her to understand the necessity of deciding something, and told her that I could not be there wasting my time and awaiting her pleasure, as she had already said she would come back, and she was simply putting it off to an indefinite period. She sent word to Tamatoa, and her relations, to come and decide for her. That evening they all arrived. My husband then spoke to them and said the French government had been very badly treated by them, and that they were keeping the queen of Tahiti amongst themselves with no good object. He also asked them whether in case the French refused to receive this queen of Tahiti any more, would they give up their government for her as a sacrifice? This seemed to frighten these men, and Tapoa said to the queen: "You had better leave. We have heard that Great Britain has withdrawn her intentions of helping you, and you had better go straight back to your own government." She said then to Tapoa: "Who will take me? I have asked for a vessel to take me home, but it appears that I cannot have one." Tapoa replied: "Ariitaimai has been here for several months awaiting your pleasure, and vessels have been here for you, but you have simply been undecided all this time. What will you do without Tahiti?" She said that as the English were the persons who brought her to this island, she expected that they would also take her back home to her island. My husband then told her that the English certainly would not put a vessel at her orders to take her home to Tahiti, and that the French had already sent their war vessel twice, and now there was still a chance of their sending a third time, only he warned her that if, at that time, she still continued to play off as she had already done, the patience of the French would be exhausted, and she would ultimately lose her possessions in the island. The queen then made some excuses by saying that her relations had been the cause of her being kept there, and that she personally had always wished to go back to Tahiti. Tapoa then got up and said that he washed his hands of all responsibility in keeping back the queen and that he himself was going to leave that evening for his island, and his final decision had been already stated. His advice was that the queen should go right back to her own country. He then saluted them and left the meeting at once. The remaining two sovereigns felt very fidgety over the decision taken by Tapoa. These two, however, still continued to decide not to let Queen Pomare leave. We then returned to our house. An hour or so afterwards we were sent for. There was then a long argument. After these discussions they decided to allow her to make her final decision in the matter. When she heard this, she cried and said: "I shall leave tomorow. I will not remain with you any more." We then went home, and my husband sent word to the captain of the vessel, which had arrived in the meanwhile, to prepare for our departure. We then left the island without the queen, and came within sight of Motuuta, when we were caught in a heavy squall, and our fore yard was broken, which forced us to return to Moorea. This action was reported to the governor, who, it seems, had thought that the queen was on board with us, and we hardly arrived in Moorea, when he came along in a steamer. My husband having seen by the signs of the flags that the governor was on board, rowed off at once to meet him. The governor then came ashore to see me, and offered to take me back to Tahiti the next morning, which I accepted. We then left our schooner behind us at Moorea.

We then remained at home in great trouble, and did not know what was to be done next. The governor on several instances offered to make me the sovereign of the island in place of Pomare, which, however, I could not entertain. We then continued to wait for the queen to decide. We passed a few weeks of peacefulness in Papeete, when one day, an old native preacher came along, and secretly gave me a letter which I at once saw was from Queen Pomare.

In this letter she wrote to say that she was very sorry for not having accepted my offer to bring her back to Tahiti, and that the news she had received from her island was troubling her a great deal, as it stated that her lands and her people were all killed or wounded, and that she had been informed that the chiefs had come in and submitted themselves to the French. This decided me at once to try again and ask the governor to allow me once more to go back to the island and get her and bring her back to us. This wish seemed to aggravate the governor towards me. He said: "Have you not done enough for the Pomares, that you should still continue to go down to fetch them?" He showed me a document which he was preparing, and which he intended to have published, by which he intended to take hold of the island and break up the act of protectorate that had been already made, and on account of my refusal to become the queen, instead of Pomare, to make the island a French colony at once. I, however, begged him to allow me to go down and bring Pomare back. He reluctantly agreed, and said to me: "You can go down, and if by chance that queen should hear you, you can bring her to Moorea, and leave her there, and let me know". We then started, on that very day. We called at Huahine, and the next morning we anchored in Raiatea. We found the queen fully prepared this time to come aboard with no more trouble, and we left there that evening. The next day we anchored in Moorea, where we went ashore. The steamer then proceeded to Papeete. The next day [6 Feb. 1847] it reappeared with the governor on board, and he came in person to receive the queen and bring her back home. As we all went on board a salute was fired. We went around the island flying the protectorate flag at the fore, to inform the people of these islands that their queen had returned. We then continued our route for Papeete, and on arriving there the forts from the shore saluted the flag. The queen remained several hours on board the steamer, as the governor wished the natives to see that the queen had really come back.

There were then in port several ships of war, French, British and American ships. There were soldiers in line on shore to receive us, and we were conducted to the governor's house. Tapoa had come with us on our return. The peace of the island was then decided upon. On arriving at the governor's house, we found all the commanders of the troops and vessels there, and before them I was thanked by Bruat for what I had done for my country.

THE END

80499413R00072

Made in the USA
Lexington, KY
03 February 2018